THE HOUSE THAT TAI MING BUILT

大明所建之屋

李金蘭著

Virginia Lee ❧ **THE HOUSE**

THAT TAI MING

BUILT ❧ THE MACMILLAN COMPANY, NEW YORK
COLLIER-MACMILLAN LIMITED, LONDON

Printed in the United States of America

THE MACMILLAN COMPANY, NEW YORK

COLLIER-MACMILLAN CANADA, LTD., TORONTO, ONTARIO

Library of Congress catalog card number: 63–15688

Contents

Part One

The Man with the Queue

A SMALL BRASS SIGN, HANGING ON BRASS LINKS FROM A steel bracket, read "Tai Ming Co., Since 1855." On cold days, when the air was brisk, the sign swung back and forth, at times in rhythm to the nearby cable car rolling down the steep hills of California Street. In September, when the days in San Francisco were warm and lovely, the sign made not a stir and it was as calm and serene as its worthy neighbor across the street, Old St. Mary's Church.

The windows of the Tai Ming Company displayed the works of the skilled craftsmen of China: potteries, porcelains, lacquer ware, enamelware, and ivories. Silk, satin, and brocade had a place to themselves and a corner of the red silk, undone from its roll, touched a *blanc-de-chine* Goddess of Mercy.

Inside were the descendants of Kwong Tai Ming, the founder of the store. The little great-great-granddaughter and great-great-grandson of Tai Ming were diligently examining a porcelain bowl with the famous rice grain pattern, both wrongly guessing that grains of rice had been

[3]

baked into the bowl, not knowing that the pattern had been achieved by incising the bowl.

The great-grandson of Tai Ming, the father of the little boy and girl playfully studying the porcelain bowl, was standing by a counter, verifying an invoice on an abacus. His slim, long fingers moved quickly, and the black balls of the abacus made a succession of pleasant clicking sounds. This great-grandson of Tai Ming was a serious man, and his hair was already gray at the sides. He was slim, of medium height and he embodied all the virtues expected of a man; he was industrious, frugal, honest and loyal.

His long, slim face was perpetually stern, and it made a false facade that concealed the deep affection he felt for his family; for indeed he cherished his son and adored his daughter; he was loyal to his wife and brother and, even now, filial to his father.

The other great-grandson of Tai Ming was by a counter at his daily chore of dusting the merchandise. The thin bamboo switch of the chicken-feather duster measured longer than his short arms. If the man across the store, his brother, was slim and stern-looking, this short, round man was his extreme opposite in appearance and temperament. Relatives and friends usually quoted a proverb when comparing these two brothers, "As in the five fingers of a single hand there are different sizes, so are the sons and daughters of a single family."

This man dusting would be the thumb, short and moon-round of face and body. His rich black hair was shiny and sleek, parted in the center and combed down flat on each side; his head looked like a juicy round apple, with a knife slash for his mouth. He was half-singing and half-humming a song of his own spontaneous composition, a happy tune, for he was a cheerful man with a mellow sense of humor, an elastic mind and an abundance of affection that overflowed for his niece and nephew.

Grandfather Kwong, the senior member of the family, was the father of the two brothers, and the grandfather of the two small children now arguing about the rice grain pattern of the porcelain bowl. Grandfather Kwong was the grandson of Tai Ming, and always deemed himself fortunate to have been able to hear from the long-deceased founder of the store first-hand stories of the Gold Rush days of California.

Grandfather Kwong was slim and well proportioned and of medium height. During his early years in San Francisco he wore long gowns or loose cotton trousers and jackets, but now he wore a western style suit. His queue had been cut off many years ago and now his full crop of hair was streaked with gray. He walked softly on soft, white-soled shoes of black cotton and his walk was slow, for his old person was calm and dignified. When young, he had been industrious; now no more a young man, industry was no longer demanded of him and he was entitled to enjoy simple daily pleasures.

Grandfather Kwong called to his grandchildren, "Kiang, Mui Mui, let us be on our way now."

The two children responded quickly, eager for their daily walk with their gentle and affectionate grandfather. It was during these hours, in the nearby park or as they strolled leisurely through the town, that stories of gold-mining days or stories of another era in earlier San Francisco flowed forth from Grandfather Kwong.

The father looked up from his abacus to see if his children had answered Grandfather Kwong. The father was satisfied with the children's behavior; had they not responded quickly they would have been reprimanded sternly. A lack of filial piety was a cardinal sin in this family.

One slim finger was erect in the air as the father said: "You two must listen to your grandfather and cause him no trouble."

The children bobbed their heads and answered distinctly, "Yes, Father." Their father was a literal man, meaning every word of his warning and the children knew it, but the fear in their hearts was small. Still, had they not been entirely respectful to Grandfather Kwong, their father would never have heard of it. In his old years Grandfather Kwong was inclined to be indulgent, yet he had once been as stern with his own children, the two brothers.

Grandfather Kwong stretched out both his hands and each child clutched at one so that the old man was in the center. Grandfather Kwong towered above the children and he looked down at them. They were not looking at him, but he smiled at them for at that moment he was a happy man: this was the good, simple life, that a man should grow old in an atmosphere of contentment. His grown sons were honest and industrious and his grandchildren sweet and filial.

Grandfather Kwong led them out of the store. The brass sign was swaying. Grandfather Kwong warned the children to button their coats. The boy did so instantly. The little girl hesitated for a fraction of a minute, thinking it was not at all cold. Yet even at her tender age she realized she had to give face to her grandfather and she buttoned her coat.

They stood on the corner of Grant Avenue and California Street, behind the Tai Ming Company, waiting for the cable car to roll down to Kearny Street. Grandfather Kwong recalled in his mind how as a young boy he had ridden up the hills in those cable cars, one hand hanging onto a pole, his queue parallel in the air, his other hand carrying an ivory chess set or a porcelain vase to deliver to a home up in Nob Hill. That had been before the fire and earthquake of 1906.

The cable car began its roll downhill, the bell clanging, and a crowd of people along with Grandfather Kwong and the two children crossed the street. They walked down California Street and within a yard from the sloping green hills of St. Mary's Square, Grandfather Kwong let go the children's hands and the two scampered off to play. Grandfather Kwong sat on a wooden bench and watched his two grandchildren jump and run. Again he was happy for it was warm in the sun and his grandchildren were healthy and full of vitality.

His grandson was named Tai Kiang, meaning One Most Brilliant. He was a bright, alert little boy who bore some resemblance to Grandfather Kwong. He was filial and doubtless would grow up to be a worthy man. But it was the little girl whom Grandfather Kwong secretly loved more dearly. He always predicted she would grow to be a beauty; he saw it in her fine, clear skin, her large, long eyes, her arched eyebrows, her symmetrical mouth and her oval face that tapered so delicately at the chin. She would always be a small person, he speculated, for her bones were narrow; perhaps like her grandmother in China. But it was not her physical appearance that made him love her more than he did his grandson. It was her love of the stories and books that were his passion now that moments of leisure were his. She was a mere child of five, but she looked for hours at the black-and-white illustrations in a novel about the ancient dynasties of China and, to his pleasure, she could guess by the pictures what the stories were about. If he taught her a character or two in the book, she would never forget them. Then too, the look of enchantment on her face when he told her the stories his grandfather old Tai Ming had told him about mining days in California gave him such satisfaction that it never bothered him that his throat was always slightly sore after almost two hours of storytelling. Again and again she would beg him for more and he would comply, and in a little while the restless grandson would walk away in the middle of a tale, and Grandfather Kwong would tell the rest of the story with his old hands holding his young granddaughter's hands.

The little girl's name was Bo Lin, Precious Lotus. Grandfather Kwong disliked the name, thinking it was entirely too common and too naïve, and he chose instead to call her Mui Mui, a term of affection meaning Little Sister. He watched her now as she hunted for small flowers while her brother hunted for ants, and remembered for the first several weeks of her life she had been called by a name of his choice, Shui Heung, Fragrance from Books. His mind wandered back to earlier days in San Francisco. Suddenly the little girl was not within sight. Grandfather Kwong cried out, "Fragrance! Where are you? Come back here within sight of me! Fragrance! Fragrance!"

The little girl's face showed up above the slope of the hill, below the bench where Grandfather Kwong sat. Instantly she got up, her face alight with unrestrained laughter. She ran toward him with both hands outstretched and took his hands roughly and said: "Grandfather, you are dreaming again. You called me Fragrance. You are crazy."

Had she been an older child it would not be permissible for her to say he was crazy, even in fun. But she was only five, and he laughed along with her.

"Did I really call you Fragrance?"

"Yes, Grandfather, you did, as you did last week."

"Where is my mind in my old days! Already I don't remember I called you Fragrance, yet you can recall I called you Fragrance last week!"

"Grandfather! Why indeed do you call me Fragrance?"

He looked at her and saw genuine interest in her face. He pulled her down to the bench to sit by him. He said, "If you really wish to know, you must be prepared for a long story."

She sat down, her child's face serious like a grown girl's.

Grandfather Kwong began: "Ngai Wah, Skillful and Beautiful; Sil Toa, Little Peach; Shui Heung, Fragrance from Books; these were the names deliberated over for you at birth. It was your father's and Second Uncle's desire to name you Skillful and Beautiful, that you would someday live up to the name and become a clever and beautiful artist. I myself was absorbed in reading the *Three Kingdoms* at that time and thought of the name Fragrance from Books, hoping you might become a writer someday.

"Your mother suggested Little Peach, for you had been very tiny at birth. To this your father, Second Uncle and I objected vigorously for it was common, as what girl is not named Orchid or Peony, or Blossom or Peach?

"Of course, in deference to me, my choice of Fragrance from Books was given you. But a few days prior to your full month after birth a letter from China arrived at our home in San Francisco. It was written at your grandmother's request. In this lengthy letter she wrote . . ." Grandfather Kwong paused before reciting what was supposed to be Grandmother Kwong's letter:

We have received the joyous news that a daughter has been born. A son first, and now a girl . . . that is indeed good. Remember always that though we need many sons to carry on our name, daughters are also precious. Teach her to be a good child, to be modest, to be filial; teach her to address her elders correctly, even her brother who is to be called by her "Elder Brother." Remember that the mother who has given birth must remain in bed for a complete month, else she will come upon old age sooner than she should. Remember also to eat the chicken and wine soup every day for it will benefit the weakened body. You write that the name Shui Heung, Fragrance from Books, has been given our new daughter. What nonsense is this that you wish a girl in our family to be a writer someday? Is that not for a man to be? Remember that in a woman virtue is preferred above talent. This girl child will be sweet and modest, and learn the arts that will make her a good wife and mother. And another thing, if the name Heung, Fragrance, is given her, would not naughty children someday in school tease her thusly: "Heung, Heung; Chuh, Chuh . . . Fragrant, Fragrant; Smelly, Smelly"? These are things men do not think of!

Now let me tell you of a strange thing that transpired. It has been a habit of mine to sit alone in the sun each morning on a stone bench by the lotus pool. Every day I look at the beautiful lotus as they stand in quiet serenity upon the pool. One morning, upon waking up after having dozed off in the sun, I saw a small lotus that had snapped off from its stem floating about the pool. It seemed to have the magical power of a goddess and as I looked in wonder, it floated all the way until it was directly in front of my feet. I cried to a servant to fetch me the lotus, and upon close inspection I found it to be an unusually beautiful pink lotus, delicate as heavenly clouds. This lovely pink lotus I had the servant set in a porcelain bulb bowl, and there in my chambers it remained.

Weeks later, your letter arrived, telling of the new daughter, explaining on what day and what hour. Immediately I recalled that it was the same day and the same hour that the pink lotus floated to my feet. Now I ask all of you, was this not some wonderful omen from Heaven! This I am certain no one will dispute. Accordingly, I advise you to name my new granddaughter Bo Lin, Precious Lotus. Precious she most certainly is, and may she always be like the lotus that symbolizes purity and perfection, for what else grows out of the mud yet does not become defiled by it and grows tall and proud in beauty and nobility!

"That, Mui Mui, concludes what your grandmother wrote!" said Grandfather Kwong.

He looked gently at the little girl, seeing the look of enchantment on her face. He resumed, in spite of a slight soreness in his throat. "Jade, Peach, Lotus, Blossom . . . what girl is not so named? Isn't the Fong girl across the street named Golden Lotus; Mrs. Chin's daughter, Precious Jade; Mr. Young's unfortunate little girl with the bad limp, Golden Orchid? At that time I was just beginning to be free enough to read every evening and the knowledge gained from books filled me with serene happiness. So I thought how good if you were to know that from books can come fragrances as sweet as perfume, and that perhaps someday you could even compose a poem or a clever story."

The little girl stared up at the sky; her eyes followed a single cloud until it was out of sight and she looked gently into her grandfather's old eyes. She sighed with regret, for indeed she loved the name Fragrance from Books, for books had always filled her with something she could not name but surely felt.

Putting a young hand on her grandfather's old hand, she asked: "Grandfather, can you call me Fragrance from Books always? Can that be done or can that not be done?"

Grandfather Kwong knew the child was completely serious and he dared not laugh. Instead he gave her much

face by replying as seriously: "Indeed that can be done.
Fragrance, call your brother over for we must go home
now. Fragrance, Fragrance, walk . . . don't run, Fragrance."

Grandfather Kwong and his grandchildren stood on
the corner to wait for the cable car to go down the hill
before crossing the street. Clear now, they crossed, Grandfather Kwong warning, "Kiang, Fragrance, hold on to
me."

The boy asked, "Who is Fragrance?"

"That's my new name, Shui Heung, Fragrance from
Books."

While Grandfather Kwong was busy looking out for
oncoming traffic, the little boy secretly called to the little
girl. He grinned at her, then stuck his tongue out; she
hoped it had nothing to do with her new name.

Throughout the rest of the day the little girl went
about the house attempting to persuade everyone to call
her by her new name. Everyone refused, but good-
naturedly, for all knew that the name had once been
the choice of the senior member of the family. However,
Grandfather Kwong kept true to his words and throughout
the evening rice he called her Fragrance.

"Fragrance, partake of some salted eggs, some mustard
greens. Fragrance . . . eat slowly, slowly."

Then came the inevitable that Grandmother Kwong
had forewarned in her letter: Kiang, with much mischief
in his eyes, his wooden chopsticks in the air, said, "Listen
everyone, I've thought of something very funny; Heung
Heung; Chui Chui; Fragrant Fragrant; Smelly Smelly."

The little girl started to cry; her lovely new name to be
defiled so! But in another second, Grandfather Kwong's

old hand was upon her young hand and he too began to laugh with the little boy. He said: "How true were the words of your grandmother! Ah, perhaps women are not so simpleheaded after all! I still do not like the names of flowers, but no more will I call you Fragrance. Mui Mui, you will always be Mui Mui to me!"

In a gesture of deep affection, Grandfather Kwong picked up a piece of pork with his chopsticks and fed the little girl. She was deeply touched and she thought secretly: What matters what my name is, as long as he is always there to call me?

THE EDGES OF THE ROOFS ON THE MAGNIFICENT HOME curved upward, as the spirit of man should always look upward. The glazed, deep blue tiles of the roofs glistened like amethyst on a bright sunny day. The adjacent garden was spacious, and within, on a hill, was an octagonal pavilion. The house had been built in accordance with the ancient belief about wind and water, and the geomancer's advice had been followed as to where and how the house should be located to assure the propitious influence of wind, earth, water and the spirits of the region.

This was a home consisting of many one-storied buildings surrounded by a high, red brick wall. Each building opened on a courtyard where flowers grew in earthen pots lined against the walls. The windows consisted of narrow strips of wood which formed a latticework covered with translucent white paper. The windows were in designs of fans and leaves, the doors in the shapes of half-moon, full moon and flower vase.

Inside, the furniture was simple in design. Many pieces

[14]

had been carved out of a solid block of wood like a piece of sculpture. In the main rooms were the conventional settings of blackwood and rosewood tables and chairs placed along the wall under fine paintings and calligraphy.

The land for the spacious garden had been acquired years after the house had been built. The original builder had loved the wall-enclosed garden more than the house. The original builder studied and read much in his late years in the small octagonal pavilion on a low hill in the garden, pausing often to look at the peach and plum trees below. Beyond was a camelback bridge, its reflection in the water making a silvery circle on the surface of the lotus pool. In a far corner, against delicate blades of heavenly bamboo, was a huge green jardiniere filled with beautiful goldfish, their trembling fins like a lovely thin haze of pure white silk.

This was the House that Tai Ming Built. This was the house erected to replace a humble house of stone and mud in a small village in south China after Tai Ming had returned a wealthy man from the foothills of the mining country of the Sierra California. This was the house Tai Ming stood and watched being built while the calluses on his hands and feet were still hard from panning and shoveling for gold in California. This was the house Tai Ming lived in with his widowed mother, both dressed in silk and satin. This was the house Tai Ming left after two years of idle living when his industrious spirit compelled him to return to California, to San Francisco. This was the house Tai Ming returned to after almost half a century in San Francisco. This was the house in which Tai Ming died.

There also, Grandfather Kwong had been born and

reared; his sons, the fat and the slim, had lived there and played in the open courtyards. There too, someday, the little girl and boy, Bo Lin and Tai Kiang, were to return.

It was autumn, 1849, when news of the discovery of gold in California reached the port cities of Hong Kong and Canton, then the nearby villages. In China, it was the Year of the Cock, the Twenty-Ninth Year of the Emperor Tao Kung. Those in the city who could afford to board ship to California hurried aboard, their meager clothing and bedding rolled into bamboo mats tucked under their arms.

Tai Ming was a boy of sixteen then, living with his widowed mother in a village near the capital of Canton. It was a small village completely surrounded by a circular growth of bamboo trees. One entered or left this village of dirt roads and small homes through a stone gateway, barred at night by five cypress poles inserted through the iron rings of the gateway.

The lives of the people living within the delicate green wall of bamboo were simple. Most of the men grew vegetables for their own use and sold the surplus. A few shopkeepers were located there: the herbalist with his remedy of brewed monkey flesh that promised to rid one of an unhealthy pallor if drunk when steaming hot; the hot bun and candy vendor; the geomancer; the metalsmith; the carpenter, and the village teacher who also wrote letters for those who could not, for a coin or two but more often in exchange for a fresh bunch of mustard greens.

When the news of the discovery of gold in California reached the village it was met with mild skepticism, for they heard, "Shake the mountain and the gold rushes forth like fire from the mouth of an angry dragon!" The hard-working villagers laughed and said, "How can wealth be so easily attained?" and continued work on their vegetable gardens.

Tai Ming pulled one large ear, saying to a neighbor: "To believe a tale like that is to believe one is the rightful successor to the Dragon Throne! Fate determines who is to be poor, who is to be wealthy; one does not cross an ocean to gain riches."

Tai Ming's neighbor nodded his head in serious agreement. A few months later, however, after Tai Ming had gone on a day's holiday to Canton, he returned home brimming with excitement, telling his mother that it was his fate to be a wealthy man.

A large portrait of Tai Ming continues to occupy a place of honor in the House that Tai Ming Built. His memory is still revered. His picture also decorates the village school, a building he donated to the villagers several years before his death. Grandfather Kwong kept a small snapshot of Tai Ming in his vest pocket, taking it out often to show to Lin and Kiang. This snapshot had been in Grandfather Kwong's pocket on the day of the fire and earthquake of 1906 in San Francisco, making it the sole remaining picture in San Francisco of Tai Ming. All others were lost on that fateful day.

Lin asked Grandfather Kwong, "Why did Great-Great-Grandfather Tai Ming wear his hair in a queue?"

Kiang said, "How funny and stupid it looks, a pigtail on a man!"

Grandfather Kwong blinked his eyes hard and said: "Ha! Funny and stupid, indeed! The words and reactions

of an ignorant person; the words and reactions of the foreigners who saw Tai Ming and his countrymen for the
first time in California. When meeting with the new, the
unexpected, the strange, learn the reasons and be enlight-
ened rather than dismiss it as stupid and thus become both
ignorant and arrogant. Ask instead, why did Tai Ming
wear a queue? Did his grandfather wear a queue, his great-
great-grandfather? Ask why I do not wear a queue? Was it
convenient to wear a queue, fashionable to wear a queue,
or what?"

Kiang's face flushed with shame. Lin suggested viva-
ciously, "There were no barbershops and he wore it in a
queue so it would not get into his food!"

Grandfather Kwong laughed and said these were not
the reasons, but nevertheless the reasoning was not entirely
bad for a five-year-old girl.

Grandfather Kwong continued: "To know why Tai
Ming wore a queue we must go back in Chinese history, to
the time when the Mongol Emperor Kublai Khan and his
successors ruled China for nearly a century in the Yuan
Dynasty from the year 1230 until 1368 A.D., when they
were driven out of power by the Chinese. A native emperor
was thus upon the throne and the native dynasty known
as the Ming Dynasty was to last from 1368 to 1644. As
always in the history of China, the founder of a new
dynasty was vigorous and brilliant but followed by weak
rulers who brought a ruling house to decay and caused the
people to rebel. Rebellion had broken out in north China
foretelling the downfall of the Mings; the ruling house had
become weak and the people suffered from taxation and
famine. Added to the rebellion had been successful attacks
upon China in the north by Manchus who continuously
pressed down toward China. From out of the people's re-

bellion stepped forth its leader who proclaimed himself
emperor and succeeded in capturing Peking. The Ming
emperor, in despair, went to the top of Coal Hill in Peking
and hanged himself.

"Now Ming soldiers and Manchu soldiers joined together to defeat the rebel leader who had proclaimed himself emperor. The rebel leader was defeated and his forces
broken up. But the Chinese Mings were not restored to
power, for the Manchus refused to go and took over the
whole Empire of China, and brought a six-year-old prince
to Peking and thus established the Ching Dynasty in the
year 1644.

"To remind every Chinese that he was a subject of the
Manchu emperor, he was forced to adopt the conquerors'
method of dressing the hair; his forehead was shaved and
his hair braided in a queue. The conquering Manchus
arranged things thus: First came the Imperial edict forbidding men to dress in the Ming style. Next came the
Imperial edict ordering all male persons to adopt the
Manchu style of trimmed forehead and queue. Because the
men resisted, barbers were dispatched to enforce the order,
carrying with them Imperial sanction to cut off any man's
head who refused. Preferring their heads to their hair, one
by one the Chinese stretched their necks to allow the
barber to shave them. So it was, two centuries after the
Manchu edict, that Tai Ming and every man and man-
child wore a queue and the hair across their forehead was
shaved clean."

"A good story, indeed!" Lin said, clapping her hands.

"History, Mui Mui, this is Chinese history."

"Grandfather, did you ever wear a queue? Why aren't
queues worn anymore by Father, Second Uncle and yourself?"

"That part of history I will tell some other time. My throat is dry and sore now."

"Grandfather, if that is too long to tell, tell about Tai Ming and how he finally came to California!"

Grandfather Kwong used a trick Tai Ming himself had often used when he wished to tell no more stories of mining days. Grandfather Kwong pretended to doze. But the story of how Tai Ming came to California was all written down on soft rice paper, bound in blue parchment and secured by vermilion silk cord. No one knew which of the generations wrote it, and it was often suggested that more than one person was the author, for the writing varied; some characters were written with bold, swift strokes, some with awkward, unsure strokes. When Lin was old enough to read, the book was taken out of a blackwood desk from the House that Tai Ming Built and shipped across the Pacific to her home in San Francisco. The words read up and down and she had no difficulty reading it for it was written in the vernacular. . . .

On a fine day in early spring, Tai Ming allowed himself the unusual luxury of a day of rest from his vegetable garden to spend a holiday in the nearby city of Canton. His queue was braided with red silk for the occasion, and his loose trousers and jacket were fresh. Journeying a short time by junk, Tai Ming arrived in Canton when the sun was directly over the crowded city. Tai Ming was excited and hungry, and jostling through the crowd he came upon a street vendor sitting upon the cobbled street, his wicker basket of hot sweet buns beside him. Tai Ming paid a coin for one of the buns and ate it standing up, staring in wild-eyed wonder at the hordes of people passing by. The beating of sticks upon pigskin drums sounded near, crashing cymbals too, and the thin sound of a stringed instrument spun through the air like the beguiling voice of a beautiful, spoiled girl. Tai Ming finished the bun and, feeling the need to moisten his throat, asked cautiously of the vendor for a cup of his tea. The vendor bade him welcome to it and Tai Ming lifted a porcelain cup immersed in a bowl filled with cool water and poured himself tea. As Tai Ming drank, his attention was attracted to a large crowd of people moving toward him. The streets of the city were indeed crowded, but this large group seemed to sway forward in a close band, some laughing, some shouting, some waving an angry fist. Tai Ming backed against a stone wall for he was frightened. The bun vendor looked up and called to Tai Ming. "Don't be frightened. Doesn't this happen in your village? It's merely a criminal and his guards on their way to the prison."

The vendor stood up and stretched his neck to see above the crowd. He pointed for Tai Ming and said, "See, there's the prisoner and he's been arrested for stealing food from the shop of Mr. Wong. Come, come, stand on your toes and see for yourself. If this is a sight you've never beheld, see now for yourself so that you'll learn what shame can be brought upon one who is not industrious and who lives by taking what doesn't belong to him."

Tai Ming stood on his toes and stretched his neck and saw in the center of the crowd the prisoner. A large bamboo mat was poked over the prisoner's head and round his neck was wound a heavy chain, extending down to his body, the end being held by a prison guard. Another solemn-faced guard carried a placard which stated the nature of the crime, and a third guard carried a brass gong which he struck with a mallet in a steady rhythm. Beads of perspiration formed on Tai Ming's forehead. He said: "Indeed, what shame it brings upon oneself and one's family to be paraded around so! If that were to happen to me I would rather not be a human being."

The bun vendor returned to his squatting position upon the cobbled street. He said, as he laid a damp cloth over the buns to protect them from flies, "Yes, young one, see and learn, for that's the purpose of this parade."

"Where do they go now?" asked Tai Ming.

"On to the prison over yonder near the river," answered the vendor.

Tai Ming followed the crowd through the narrow streets. The horde of people wove through twisted alleyways, passing dingy buildings and piled garbage such as Tai Ming had never seen in his own village. An old woman pulled the long queue of the prisoner, sending the crowd into a state of near-hysterical laughter. On and on Tai Ming followed the crowd until suddenly they came upon a street lined with open shops of a brilliance such as he had never seen before. He stopped and stared in utter fascination but the impatient horde of people pushed him on. Tai Ming saw hanging above him huge gold-and-red lacquer signs; for a breathless second he caught a fleeting glimpse of a gilded Buddha sitting happily upon the counter of a crowded bazaar; for another brief moment he stared in a hynoptic trance at a brilliant red silk a merchant was tenderly folding for a shrewd old woman. By now Tai Ming had lost interest in the further fate of the prisoner and began to edge sideways away from the crowd. His toes were trampled on, his shoulders and head buffeted, but at last he managed to press his body against a wall while the crowd surged past him. A long trail of laughing children, some running barefoot and shouting in a high chorus, "Thief! Thief!" brought up the tail of the hurrying mob and Tai Ming relaxed and wiped his moist face with his wrinkled sleeves. He looked about him, enchanted by what he saw, for now he was in the ancient quarters of the merchants and craftsmen of Jade Street. There was the never-ending music of the city again, pervading the bazaars. It came from afar and the distance lent the stringed instrument a more subdued tone so that what had been the beguiling voice of a spoiled girl was now the plaintive voice of a lovely courtesan.

Tai Ming was standing in front of the Shop of a Hundred Gems and before his eyes were snuff bottles, incense burners, bulb bowls, vases, sprays of flowers, jewelry and hair ornaments all carved from the purest of pure green jade. He pointed to a jade ring and asked the shopkeeper the price. And the shopkeeper, knowing that Tai Ming was but a village bumpkin, quoted the price with the greatest nonchalance. "Ah, it's too dear," replied Tai Ming, for the price was more than what he earned in a year. And the shrewd shopkeeper, thinking perhaps that there was a possibility of a sale to the village bumpkin said: "Jade is indeed dear for jade is precious. Perhaps some of these will serve: pieces carved from rock crystal, amber, turquoise, jasper, amethyst or coral." Indeed, to Tai Ming's untrained eyes these were as beautiful as jade but again the prices were beyond his means. Tai Ming walked away from the Shop of a Hundred Gems slowly, for he could not take his eyes from all the lovely things. Onward through the stone cobbled streets he moved, going from the Shop of the Thousand Jade Buddhas to the Shop of the Jade Brush Pot for the Scholar until he had walked through all the shops of Jade Street.

Now Tai Ming was viewing the splendors of Ivory Street. He saw upon the counters wise old men of ivory, their long whiskers hanging down to robes carved in the most delicate flowing lines. He shyly peeped through the open doorway of a craftsman's shop and saw an ivory carver scraping and chiseling a three-foot tusk, and still another craftsman polishing with pumice powder and a damp cloth, a finished ivory screen upon which were carved the Flowers of the Four Seasons. He saw an ivory ball proudly held by the master craftsman who had spent months in creating it and who now called the village bumpkin Tai Ming to enter to see the masterpiece. Before Tai Ming's startled eyes, the craftsman demonstrated that within this ivory ball were many other balls one inside the other, each rolling free from every other, showing different lacelike patterns as they turned. And this, the master craftsman told Tai Ming, had all been carved from one solid block of ivory.

On and on Tai Ming went, to Silk Street, Embroidery Street, Fan Street, Lacquer Street, Goldsmith Street, Porcelain Street, Lantern Street, discovering for the first time the amazing workmanship of his countrymen. Here and there through the narrow streets, towering above the little shops in the background were the beautiful temples and pagodas of ancient Canton.

Again he bought a bun from a vendor, and peanuts from another vendor. He guessed that he should be on his way home now. With a deep sigh he started off to board the junk that would take him back to his village. But still the big city fascinated him as now the goods of the marketplace tempted and teased him. Rich red pork sausages specked with dark liver strung together with red strings

hung on stalls, as did dried salt fish and sumptuous roast
ducks, their colors as deep and red as lacquer ware. Bushels
and bushels of green and yellow-tipped bean sprouts com-
plemented the baskets of mustard greens next to them;
upon a wooden shelf were jars of salted ducks' eggs, each
egg encrusted with gray earth; there were brown earthen
jars of soya sauce, oyster sauce, brown bean curd and black
bean curd. In awe Tai Ming wandered through the shops
of the food merchants until he discovered that he had
strayed far from where he had intended to go for the junk.
He hurried, frightened now, for he was not familiar with
the city, and the time was approaching when he should be
on his way home.

He came upon a riverfront but knew it was not the
narrow river that had brought him to the city. Instead this
was a waterway, li and li long and as wide, and upon the
water were junks, sampans, rafts, houseboats and paddle
boats. Here again was another spectacle to capture his
attention: a gang of men on a paddle boat powered by the
strong thrust of their bare feet upon the paddle blades; a
woman with feet as ugly and as large as a man's bending
over her houseboat to snatch back her child who had
stumbled into the water; huge, frightful-looking eyes
boldly painted on the prows of junks. On and on Tai
Ming walked, his senses acutely offended by the stench of
life upon the river although at times the aroma of salt fish
steaming in hot rice whiffed out from a houseboat.

Suddenly before his startled eyes loomed the largest
boat he had ever seen in his life; never before had he seen
such a tremendous object upon water. It was not powered
by barefoot men or rolled by large-foot women, and there
were strange writings on it totally unlike the ones that he

was accustomed to read up and down the page. All about him men, women and children looked on with enthusiasm.

A prosperous-looking man turned to Tai Ming and asked: "How can it be possible that a huge boat like that can sail across the Pacific Ocean? Yet this foreign boat has come all the way here without sinking to the bottom of the ocean!"

Tai Ming asked, "Sir, where is this boat from and what is it doing here?"

The man replied: "This boat is from a country called California, and do you see that crowd of men over there? They will board the boat soon for California, and it is said they will be back in several months richer than any of us merchants in Canton. Ah, if I were but twenty years younger, I too would go. You, young man . . ."

But Tai Ming had walked away abruptly and was running excitedly to see at a closer range the first man being admitted to board the boat. Several hundred men seemed to be filing on board, each with a small bundle tucked under his arm.

Soon the boat started on its voyage; farewells were shouted back and forth. The crowd began to disperse but Tai Ming remained where he had been standing for the past hour. Suddenly one word loomed heavily in his mind: fate, fate, fate; it was fate that had led him to wander through the alleyways, to the bazaars, to the food market and from there to get lost; fate had destined that he should know of this monster boat. He too would one day board it and sail for the country where one need only shake the mountain and the gold gushed forth like blood from the open throat of a freshly killed chicken.

With the aid of a beggar, Tai Ming found his way to his own narrow river and boarded the junk. He arrived in his village just as the first cypress pole was being inserted through the metal rings of the stone gateway.

After the evening rice the following night Tai Ming explained to his mother the long story of how fate had led him to the boat, and that certainly it was destined for him to go to California to claim his share of wealth. But his mother voiced skepticism about the gold and distrust of a barbarian country and besought him to be a dutiful son and think no more of the whole affair. Tai Ming went on to tell her that he intended to save all his money and then borrow the rest from a guild to finance his trip. His mother argued with him, saying, "A man's every cup of wine and every piece of meat are predestined; wealth is fated, and not to be had by striving."

Tai Ming replied, "Perhaps we are fated for a new era and our time of prosperity is due. I feel that as surely as I feel the breeze that stirs in the air."

Then Tai Ming's mother cried, and said, "Who will care for me if you leave?"

He replied: "Do not worry. Everything is determined by fate. When it is time for our good fortune to come, even our poorest pottery will have the tone of a jade bell for then every detail of our life will be blessed."

Tai Ming redoubled his efforts to make his garden yield its maximum. He and his mother ate less so that Tai Ming would have more vegetables to take to the neighboring village to sell. The small coins with the square hole in the center were ceremoniously dropped into a black wine vessel each evening and the pile mounted slowly but steadily. At times it seemed to the impatient Tai Ming that he would never save enough for passage to California, but just at a moment of deep discouragement, help came in the person of Tai Ming's wealthy uncle from Canton.

Uncle Ming Wah's queue glistened. He wore a long silk gown, and fanned himself ceremoniously with a brown silk fan. In sharp contrast to his wealthy uncle, Tai Ming, with his dusty queue and soiled cotton clothes, sat opposite him; beside Tai Ming, stood his mother.

This was the first meeting between nephew and uncle; the first meeting between brother-in-law and sister-in-law in sixteen years' time. An hour ago, Ming Wah had dismounted from a vehicle pulled by a swift runner, surprising his sister-in-law by his appearance at her humble home. Very nervously she had bade him welcome and served him tea, every second apologizing for its inferior quality and for her poor surroundings until Ming Wah said with pomp, making a long sweeping gesture with his fan as he talked: "I am your husband's brother, and we were both born of humble parents. There is no need to apologize."

Tai Ming's mother laughed nervously. She said, "Both born of humble parents, yes, yet I am here and you are one of the richest men in Canton."

Short, portly and smooth-skinned, Ming Wah grinned, for it pleased him enormously when people exclaimed that he was a wealthy man. He fanned himself with quick, small strokes, his round chin up, his face still fixed in a happy grin. He said, "Sister-in-Law, my fortune is slowly dwindling. To maintain a splendid house, three wives, twenty children and as many servants is gradually eating away all I have!"

"Nonsense, it is reputed your fortune is so great it will be several hundred years before any descendants of yours need to work!"

Ming Wah laughed, his brown silk fan waving in motion to his rippling laughter. "Not so, Sister-in-Law, assuredly not so!"

"That is the saying in our village."

Ming Wah laughed again, pleased that he had such a reputation. He said, "Fantastic how the common people can guess so correctly from such long range!" He roared with laughter. Then he jerked his left hand suddenly and raised it to his smooth forehead. Now his face was entirely serious, as if his hand had erased his laughter.

He began, lightly slapping a knee occasionally with his folded silk fan as he talked, "You two are unaware of the fact that over yonder beyond the Pacific is a barbarian country where gold has been discovered. Gold! Gold! Gold! Gold is everywhere there! Floating in the river, tumbling from the hills, beneath the earth, perhaps even pouring from the skies! Why heaven has ordained that the gold should be located there rather than in our own country is incomprehensible to me. I suppose it is because heaven expects some measure of effort, such as crossing the Pacific Ocean, since heaven has already been so kind as to scatter the gold so generously. If you two could have afforded to come to either Canton or Hong Kong, you would have seen the many men lining up to get on board foreign ships to go claim the gold!

"Now then, I have a proposal to make! I wish to make a gift offer of a sum of money sufficient enough for ship fare to and back, and for subsistence while there."

Tai Ming's mother was about to say they knew all about the gold and that she did not want Tai Ming to leave home but Ming Wah, thinking that she was overcome by his generous offer, smiled benevolently and motioned her to let him continue talking.

"Do not be overwhelmed by this offer. Do not credit me with being generous, for it is only a minute fraction of my wealth I give you. Were I truly a generous man should not

I have been more charitable with the profits from my many business enterprises when my brother—your husband—was alive. But no! I neglected you, my brother, my nephew. While I dined on chicken and wine, you supped on gruel and greens. While I paraded around in satin and changed to silk for bed, you worked in coarse cotton and retired to bed in the same. How unfair! Yet my brother and I were born of the same mother, our rice was spooned out of the same bowl, our tea poured from the same pot! For the sake of my conscience, in memory of my departed brother, give me face by accepting this offer!"

Tai Ming was on his feet, his face glowing with joy. He thanked his uncle profusely. But Tai Ming's mother's mind was not made up. She dreaded the thought of her son in a strange country and herself living alone. What would be worse, however, was to make Ming Wah lose face by refusing his offer. Now it was a choice between her fears or of offending Ming Wah. She preferred to yield to Ming Wah and answered nervously: "Thank you for your kindness. How can we ever hope to repay you. Tai Ming's father must be exceedingly happy at this moment."

Tai Ming, who was the soul of honesty, now blurted out that they knew all about the gold and pointed to the wine vessel containing the coins. Tai Ming's mother sighed with displeasure, for it was proper that they should have pretended ignorance as Ming Wah had assumed, thus giving face to the uncle's presumptions, however erroneous they were.

It was as Tai Ming's mother suspected, for she saw a momentary look of displeasure on Ming Wah's face, but in another second, he slapped the silk fan on his knee and said loudly and good-humoredly, "To wait until the coins accumulated to the top of the wine vessel through your vegetable peddling would be like waiting for cold water to boil by blowing hot breath into it—never!"

Ming Wah laughed uproariously at his clever simile. Tai Ming also laughed and his mother pretended to laugh.

Ming Wah opened his silk fan and fanned his forehead; talking and laughing had made him perspire. He looked at Tai Ming and said, "Tai Ming! Tai Ming! Let me look at you, let me look at you! You are well built! Not too tall but well proportioned throughout. You have good features and appear honest! You look like my tenth child. You and your mother must come and meet the family soon! Perhaps the day of your departure!"

He paused and looked toward the ceiling, a reminiscent look on his face. He said, once again facing Tai Ming, "Tai Ming, do you know that you almost became my son?"

"Really?" asked Tai Ming. His mother was embarrassed that the matter should be brought up now, the matter that had caused the rift between the two brothers.

Ming Wah's face was lit with benevolence as he told Tai Ming the story, "You see, Tai Ming, after my eighth child was born, adding only another girl to my family, I was desperate for a son. My first wife said, only stay with me and heaven will grant us a son. My second wife said, leave the others alone; preserve your energy for ourselves and we will have a son. So what did I do? I left both of them alone . . . for a while! Then my third wife was expecting a child. I was hopeful it would be a son. The cleverness of that woman, for what did she do? She went to your mother who at that time was carrying you. My third wife and your mother and father planned if a girl were born to my third wife and a son to your parents, the babies would be switched for the exchange of a small fortune!

"Well then, of course, you were born and ours was

another girl. Your mother and father refused to go through with the exchange. I discovered the plot and demanded that the original bargain be kept. Your mother and father refused, for they loved you, which was the way it should be. So, Tai Ming, that incident caused two brothers to become strangers."

Now the mother was no longer embarrassed by the story and she volunteered: "Of course, your sons began arriving after the ninth daughter. Such is fate!"

Ming Wah sighed, and said: "Such is fate, one son after the other. Eleven sons in all. At times I wonder whether my eleven sons are rewards or punishments, for the fourth, fifth and sixth sons are such rascals!"

Ming Wah rose from his chair. He slapped his back with his fan. "Tai Ming, I shall send someone over with money and instructions tomorrow. Prepare to leave next week. The sooner gone the sooner returned."

"It has not occurred to me how long Tai Ming will be in that foreign country."

Ming Wah pursed his lips, then said, "I presume in a month's time or two he will have got enough, don't you think?"

In a burst of exultation Tai Ming shouted, "With all that gold, two months will be more than enough!"

A week later, from the port city of Canton, Tai Ming boarded a foreign ship for California. His mother, his uncle and several of his uncle's small sons bade him luck and farewell. It was an ignorant but happy Tai Ming who waved farewell in return. Fortunate it was that he was ignorant, for had he known of the hardships, and worse yet, the humiliations he was to face, the journey might never have been taken.

In California it was autumn: the year 1850.

GRANDFATHER KWONG HAD JUST FINISHED READING ALOUD
a letter at the dining table to the family. Brushed down on
soft rice paper, the black characters reading up and down
told that the money forwarded from San Francisco had just
been received. It added that everyone in the House that
Tai Ming Built was well. It suggested that Lin's measure-
ments be taken so that a jacket and trousers of powder-
pink silk with a multicolored sequin design of flowers
could be handmade for her in Canton. It reminded Fook,
the round-faced one of the two brothers, that he was due
to sail for China soon. A bit of gossip was inserted; the
pitiful village idiot had departed from this earth, at last
sparing his old mother any further grief. It ended that it
was indeed unfortunate that the mother's trip to China
with Lin and Kiang had once again been postponed and,
for that reason, the letter emphatically stated, their Chinese lessons must not be neglected!

Grandfather Kwong put down the letter dictated but
not written by Grandmother Kwong. He said in all seri-

ousness: "Indeed the lessons will not be neglected! We are Sons of Tong, our home the Hills of Tong, our language the words of Tong!"

At one time in history China believed that she was the only important and civilized country in the world and claimed that all others surrounding her were barbarians. She proudly named herself the Middle Kingdom, and her subjects were people of the Middle Kingdom.

The time of the Tong Dynasty, or T'ang Dynasty, which lasted from the years 618 to 907 A.D., was a brilliant era for the Middle Kingdom during which time the Chinese empire expanded, peace and prosperity were enjoyed and art and literature reached great heights. In remembrance of that golden period those in the South began to call themselves Sons of Tong, their country the Hills of Tong, and the word "Tong" was substituted as a description for anything pertaining to the Middle Kingdom. So even to this day, in daily conversation, whenever Grandfather Kwong or any other Chinese away from his native land talked of home, he was talking about his village home in the Hills of Tong; when old he returned to the Hills of Tong, and if he should die in a foreign country, his bones were shipped back to be buried in the Hills of Tong . . . because he was a Son of Tong.

Grandfather Kwong took a sip of tea. He said, looking at his grandchildren, "If you two had returned home to the Hills of Tong two or three years ago, one of you could have written the letter for Grandmother, who neither reads nor writes."

Sun, the serious-looking father of the children, said: "A teacher has been highly recommended to me whom I shall see tomorrow. He is a man willing to spend some

time on the classics. I rather suspect Kiang has forgotten
the several months of lessons he received earlier this year;
thus there will be no need for separate lessons."

Kiang so far had had three teachers, and each one had
"returned home." This would be the first teacher for Lin.

The mother of the children, Fay, had just finished
reading the letter which was now being passed on to the
adults. "I remember that village idiot. His mouth was
slanted and he looked as if he had no nose. He couldn't
talk and he went about shrugging his shoulders all the
time."

Fook, his round face smiling, asked: "I wonder what
flowers are in bloom right now. Lin, it would be an experience for you to see the flowers: peonies, azaleas, chrysanthemums and that marvelous winter lily narcissus. We grow
our flowers in the courtyards and when they are in bloom
we set them throughout the house and the garden. In the
garden we have our plum and peach trees, their blossoms
startlingly beautiful in the wind against a background of
swaying bamboo leaves. You will never see a lotus in San
Francisco; someday you will see them from the pavilion
in the garden. And Kiang, you will like the huge goldfish;
you will stare at them all day and night and try to catch
them when their eyes are shut, but their huge, bulging
eyes never close; they just keep swimming and swimming
around in the pond in the garden. And Kiang, someone in
our village makes beautiful kites. He made one for me
once, a large, brightly colored carp with eyes that moved."

The adults were suddenly quiet, each one remembering
life in the House that Tai Ming Built. The children were
also quiet, Kiang thinking of a paper carp in the air, Lin
dreaming of plum blossoms in the winter wind.

Silence was broken. Grandfather Kwong asked Fook: "Your trip is scheduled for next month, only two weeks away. Have you made reservations for sailing?"

"Tomorrow I shall go down to the steamship company."

"What class this time?" asked Sun, the serious-faced one.

"Oh, third class. We will save on my fare so when Lin and Kiang sail, they will go in style—first class."

The liner Fook was to sail on would pull out of Pier 46 in San Francisco; it would be autumn when he arrived in the House that Tai Ming Built; crimson, pure white and bronze chrysanthemums would then be in bloom.

But now it was autumn, the year 1850, and it was a windy day. The ship that carried Tai Ming and hundreds of his countrymen finally arrived in San Francisco and dropped its anchor where it could in the overcrowded waters. A bewildered and seasick Tai Ming, his hands clutching his small possessions of clothing and bedding wrapped in a bamboo mat, was ferried to shore in a small rowboat for a fee. The new arrivals from China were met by a young representative from a Chinese mutual benefit association, the Kong Chow Association. They were directed to horse-drawn carriages and driven to the association headquarters in "Little China." There, Tai Ming's name, the name of his village and all pertinent information about him were taken and brushed onto an account book.

In 1850, San Francisco was a raw and ugly town. The water was jam-packed with deserted boats, many of them rotting away. Huge rats were everywhere, nibbling at the stacks of food stored outdoors. Tents and wooden shacks far outnumbered the few brick buildings. People from all over the world tramped the muddy streets; in places the mud was so deep it reached one's knees. Old ships, pulled out of the dirty water and beached, were used as stores and warehouses; parts of their cabin quarters called themselves "restaurants." But it mattered not to Tai Ming that San Francisco was dirty or that the foreigners he saw for the first time in such numbers secretly frightened him, for he was only to spend the night there in a muslin-partitioned hotel room. The next day he was to leave for the mining country.

With a group of Chinese, Tai Ming boarded a steamboat to sail up the bay to Stockton and from there to take a stagecoach to the mines. Heading the group was Mr. Fong, who was acting as interpreter and who was also delivering mail to the Chinese miners in the various camps. It was a harshly uncomfortable ride on the stagecoach while the drivers cursed the freight-loaded pack-mule trains that crowded the difficult, narrow roads. Mr. Fong called attention with pride to the many white men trudging on foot to the mines, who could not afford the price of a ride.

The first outfit Tai Ming purchased was a pair of heavy leather boots, a pickaxe, a shovel and a wooden bowl. After digging into the ground he filled his bowl with the dirt, added water and kneaded the two ingredients together. Any large stones were thrown out. Then the bowl was thrust under a stream of water and the dirt and small stones gradually washed away until nothing except the heavy gold remained. This was placer gold: fragments of gold that were to be found along the channels of rivers, intermixed with sand, gravel and stones. Many found it in fine gold dust, some in solid fragments. These fragments were the result of erosion that had torn the gold away from solid veins once firmly embedded in the surrounding rocks, then carried down by the rivers and in the process reduced in size by the grinding action of the debris carried by the flowing water.

In his ignorance Tai Ming had thought that in two months' time he would have "gathered" all the gold he needed. For three long years he stayed in the mining country; three years of indomitable patience and indefatigable industry.

GRANDFATHER KWONG CALLED HIS GRANDCHILDREN FOR their daily walk a little earlier than usual this afternoon. Lin and Kiang came to him, happy and eager. Little Lin took Grandfather Kwong's hand and put it against her face. The gesture touched him. He looked down at his grand-daughter; soon there would be no more of these walks, not for a while at least; every day he was giving more and more of his time to these simple excursions.

Sun, the serious-faced father, looked up from his abacus and with a stern finger in the air, softly warned, "Do not give your grandfather any trouble." He had been very busy lately, for Fook was now across the Pacific in China, in the House that Tai Ming Built. Grandfather Kwong nodded his head as if in agreement to a sound argument: that is as it should be; discipline must come from the father so that grandparents may enjoy the company of unspoiled, filial grandchildren.

Grandfather Kwong felt his pocket to make certain he had not forgotten the two bags of spicy ginger. These he would give to Lin and Kiang when they were out of sight of their father whom Grandfather Kwong knew secretly protested that ginger was too hot for children.

Today Grandfather Kwong decided they would walk up the steep hills of California Street, beyond the Chinese quarters, to Nob Hill. As the street grew steeper, the three of them at times walked backward, looking down toward the bay.

Grandfather Kwong said: "When I was a young boy I made many deliveries of such things as an ivory chess set up here. Many Sons of Tong were cooks up here and they often told me stories of their employers. The funniest one I ever heard was when this cook took a cleaver in his hand to chase away his employer's daughter, who had bothered him too much while he was busy in the kitchen. And the family, instead of dismissing him, implored him to stay and sent the daughter away, for he was an excellent chef and the daughter was totally unmanageable."

As the trio walked on they met Mr. Wong coming out of the tradesmen's entrance of an apartment house. He had worked almost twenty-five years as a cook for the same couple but soon he was due to retire and return "home."

Grandfather Kwong greeted Mr. Wong with enthusiasm and told his grandchildren to play close by while he and Mr. Wong chatted. "Mr. Kwong, Mr. Kwong, I hear you are sailing home soon. I, too, am returning. My employer made me a gift of a first-class passage fare and I am due to board ship in three days. Ah, won't it be fine to return to the Hills of Tong!"

Grandfather Kwong and Mr. Wong continued their conversation, then bade each other farewell, promising they would meet in the Hills of Tong. Grandfather Kwong called his grandchildren and they proceeded on their way home, descending the steep streets of Nob Hill.

They were now on level ground, nearing their home. As they walked Grandfather Kwong told Kiang and Lin what the city was like before the fire and earthquake of 1906. He himself on that fateful day had been wakened out of bed by a porcelain figure that fell on his head. The days to follow had been spent across the bay in Oakland, unhappy days, for the Tai Ming Company had been totally destroyed by the fire.

The three paused to rest. The brilliant sun attracted Lin. She looked at it with squinting eyes, then raised a small finger in the air to sketch it. Grandfather Kwong observed her. In a few seconds her hands stretched out to him and she said: "Grandfather, I have made a sketch for you. It is called, 'The Sun Is Noble.'" He was both amazed and touched, and he too stretched out his hands to accept the imaginary painting she offered him. He looked at her and at that moment he prayed that he would live long enough to see what this child would become.

The three resumed their walk. They were only one steep hill away from home. Grandfather Kwong looked across his left shoulder. He recalled further old experiences. He said, "Perhaps this is the time to tell you children how the Chinese finally discarded the queue."

He began: "Dr. Sun Yat Sen, the father of the Chinese revolution, lived in exile in San Francisco for a time. He lived in a hotel a little beyond the Chinese quarters on that street directly in front of us. It was not at all a grand hotel and his small room was very plainly furnished. I was a very young man then and one afternoon I took up an hour of his time talking to him about your great-great-grandfather Tai Ming. Of course later on I realized I should not have taken so much time to talk of our family, but he was a good man and he seemed to enjoy what I was telling him.

"Over in that restaurant, we merchants gave Dr. Sun a dinner. During that dinner every merchant stood up to pledge a donation for the revolution to overthrow the Manchus. I sat across from Dr. Sun and saw tears in his eyes. And do you believe it, Dr. Sun passed up many dishes of chicken and duck and squab for plain vegetables and fish?"

Down the steep hill they walked. "There at that street corner Dr. Sun aroused our feelings and received our support by calling out, 'Down with the rule of the corrupt Manchus!' We proudly raised the banner of the Nationalist party high in the air and all of us shouted with him, 'Down with the rule of the corrupt Manchus!'

"On October 10, in 1911, when news reached us in San Francisco that the revolution in China had broken out in Wuchang, I left the store in the care of a clerk to hurry over to Dr. Sun's hotel. His room was crowded with people and when I managed to get in, there was Dr. Sun in the center of the room, happy but calm and collected. Ah, the last time I saw him he was in an overcoat and a derby hat, on his way to China to lead the revolution. He shook my hand and gave me many thanks for my donations and said that now I must cut off my queue for China would again be ruled by Chinese. Yes, the queue had been worn in subjection for over two hundred years!"

They were now back at the Tai Ming Company. Kiang went off to play but Lin followed Grandfather Kwong who was resting in the back office. He knew that she wanted a story, but he wanted to rest so he took from his pocket some pieces of candy and the picture of Tai Ming which she always liked to look at. She studied the picture as she unwrapped the candy.

She said seriously, "Didn't you once tell me Tai Ming said of the white people who came to the store that he understood them by the expressions in their eyes; that the white people squinted their eyes when disapproving, shifted their eyes when merely looking with no intentions of buying, and giggled or sighed when they liked what they saw?"

Grandfather Kwong laughed; the child's memory was remarkable! "Indeed that was how Tai Ming understood them, for he knew very little English." The child continued to look serious. He looked at her, thinking . . . could not fate be kind and let nothing interfere, when next year the children and their mother planned to return to the Hills of Tong.

Suddenly she looked up and said, "Grandfather, you and Great-Great-Grandfather Tai Ming look alike! Tai Ming was as handsome as you are handsome. Surely anyone can see that!"

Grandfather Kwong became as serious as his granddaughter. He said, "If you say so, then surely it must be so." He sighed and felt a glow of pleasure, for this was the first time anyone had ever told him he was handsome. He sighed again, thinking in all probability he would never hear such flattery again. He took from his granddaughter's hands the picture photographed in San Francisco of old Tai Ming dressed in a long gown, his forehead shaved clean, his long hair in a queue, sitting in a pose as stiff as the vase of artificial flowers at his side.

The icy-cold mountain waters of California soaked through Tai Ming's leather boots, and the hot sun beat down upon his body in painful contrast to his numbed feet. The young, disillusioned gold miner had learned that gold did not float magically on the surface of the waters so that he needed only to gather it up. He had learned that he had to dig, shovel, and pan for long, agonizing hours, and if he were lucky, he weighed in an ounce of gold dust at the end of the day. Or, worse still, he sat for monotonous hours in partnership with another miner working on a "cradle," an oblong box mounted on rockers. There was no endboard to this box and at its head a sieve was attached and along the bottom of the cradle cleats were nailed. Through a process of flowing water and what seemed endless rocking, the gold in the dirt poured into the cradle piled up in little drifts behind the cleats.

It was autumn, 1850, when Tai Ming began digging in the mines. He stayed close to his countrymen and they pitched their tents by each others', cooked, ate and planned together.

Unlike his great-great-granddaughter the white men did not think Tai Ming was handsome; rather, they thought he was a ludicrous figure. But if Tai Ming offended a white miner's eyes, it wholly suited the white man that the man with the queue was meekness and yieldingness personified. The white man announced that he had priorities to all new diggings, and the man with the queue obeyed. Only after the white man had given up the claim as worthless did the man with the queue start digging; and with infinite patience he dug on and on. So the white miners, ever jealous of new gold, left "John Chinaman" alone, for they were certain the yellow man's yield would never be enough to stir their jealousy or regret.

At the time of Tai Ming's arrival, antiforeign feeling was directed against the Chileans, the Peruvians, and the Sonorans, many of whom had arrived in the mining country as early as the autumn of 1848, the year when gold was first discovered. In time these hostile feelings on the part of the native Americans and Anglo-Saxon immigrants were enlarged to cover all foreigners. Hostilities concentrated mainly against the Chinese, for they found gold in abandoned claims because they were industrious and patient—and the Americans charged that that was not justifiable. In the City the Chinese controlled the restaurant and laundry businesses and the Americans charged that that was not justifiable. The Americans and Anglo-Saxon immigrants said there were too many Chinese in the mines and took to killing, robbing and torturing them, and said it *was* justifiable, for while the men with the queues took the gold out of the white man's country they never spent it in the white man's country. In truth the Chinese faithfully paid monthly a heavy foreign miner's tax. The white men burned the Chinese laundries, toppled the idols off their temples, slashed off their queues, and the Chinese never retaliated, for they were by nature peaceful and yielding . . . and because they had never quite got over their initial fear of the hulking white men who towered above them.

By the light of an oil-burning lamp Tai Ming wrote letters to his wealthy uncle Ming Wah in Canton, telling of the hardships he and others like him were enduring. In exchange for shaving his forehead, plucking his eyebrows, and plaiting his queue, Tai Ming wrote letters for those Sons of Tong who neither read nor wrote. What others

dictated to him he wrote on coarse paper with an un-
sharpened pencil. The letters told of desperate longing
for home, the brutalities of the foreigners, the good fortune of being able to eat rice and salt fish supplied by
Chinese merchants in the nearby towns.

During the last months of his stay in California, gold
miner Tai Ming worked as a laborer, dumping cars in an
American-owned quartz mine, for it had become increas-
ingly difficult to profitably wash for gold. Though he
worked harder and longer than a white man doing the
same job, like other Chinese laborers, he earned only half
what the white man earned.

So with indomitable patience and indefatigable industry, Tai Ming sayed on. But there came the day when the
insults were too cutting, the treatment too humiliating,
when politicians began to shout, "American gold for Americans!" and demanded expulsion of the Chinese from the
mines, and the white men responded and drove the
Chinese away from claims and towns. So with bitterness
Tai Ming decided to leave California forever. He felt no
gratitude toward the country where he had been able to
line his pockets with gold, by now enough for him to
return home and live in comfort for the rest of his life.
His hands once smooth were coarse and lined with deep
ridges that would never close. His left arm just above the
elbow bore a deep scar from the wound of a knife a
drunken white miner had wielded suddenly; quite miracu-
lously the white miner had dropped to the ground in a
stupor before he was able to inflict any further harm.
Burning hatred seared Tai Ming's breast for all the white
men of this barbarian country. So in September, 1853,
almost three years from the date he first landed in San
Francisco, Tai Ming took ship to return home to China.

As the hills of the city faded from his sight, he spat upon the ocean, turned his back on the scene and, as if a silk curtain had fallen, closed his mind forever on America and began to think only of his peaceful, quiet village and the magnificent home he planned to build there.

THE BRASS SIGN OF THE TAI MING COMPANY SWUNG WITH the wind and the rain, for it was winter in San Francisco. All the shades in the windows were pulled down, and the front door locked from within. Inside, in a corner where were displayed the brass candlestick holders and the wicker baskets, a bright light shone down on the family grouped beside one of the glass counters.

All eyes were upon a package wrapped in coarse white paper that Sun, the serious-faced father, was opening. The wrapping paper unfolded to reveal a large box of deep blue. The box was secured in the center by a small, slender ivory stick inserted through a lower loop. Sun pulled the stick out of the loop. The cover of the box opened like the cover of a book. At once a chorus of "ah's" sounded, even from Sun. The object of praise was lifted out of the box by Sun, his slender fingers holding it lightly and carefully so as not to damage the precious item.

It was of the softest pink, a fitted tunic and loose trousers for Lin, the scalloped edges emphasized with gold sequins. Two sequin peacocks adorned the blouse, one in front, another in back, in iridescent colors of green, blue, gold and red. Upon each shoulder there were sequin butterflies with outstretched blue-and-green wings, and on the stiff, high collar, pastel sequin flowers. The costume glittered in the light and even Sun chuckled, for it was dainty and lovely.

The tunic was passed around. The mother, Fay, stroked the silk with her hands and marveled that the silk lining was as good as the outer material. She said, as she passed it on to Grandfather Kwong, "It is only in the Hills of Tong that such lovely handwork could be found."

The tunic lay on Grandfather Kwong's outstretched arms and he looked at it as if it were a newborn baby, half expecting such fragility would break if he were not careful. He said, "These old eyes have never seen anything so pretty." He looked at Lin, who had been standing by his side. He sat down on a wooden stool so that Lin was at eye level with him. He said, "Look, look, Mui Mui, does this please you? Kiang, come and look; perhaps a silk gown for you someday."

Kiang said he would rather have a kite in the design of a carp with eyes that moved. Grandfather Kwong's old hands trembled slightly as he laughed, and the peacock's iridescent blue-and-green tail shimmered.

Sun inspected the lovely blue box, speculating that Fook had found it somewhere and had used it instead of the box supplied by the dress shop. He said suddenly, "There is something more yet. Can it be? Can it be?"

All eyes were upon the box as Sun lifted the cloth that had covered the costume. Underneath was another wrapping and upon unfolding it, a bright vermilion red burst forth, again with iridescent sequins in all colors. This costume was a loose-fitting jacket and trousers with designs of flowers covering the entire costume, fully lined with fine red silk. A pair of matching red slippers lay to one side, and on the other, a tiny fan with a red silk tassel; tucked in a corner was a cluster of artificial flowers made to wear in the hair.

Lin's hands were clasped together against her small breast. Her happiness was ineffable, her face dreamlike. Then she was suddenly brilliant with laughter and her hands clapped spontaneously.

Again Sun lifted the costume up as carefully as he had the first one. He asked, "I wonder who made this selection?"

Fay, the mother, said: "I believe Second Uncle selected them. Who but Second Uncle would think of slippers, fan and headdress. It was indeed good of him to have done so."

Grandfather Kwong laid the pink costume on his lap. He pulled Lin to his side. He said, "Mui Mui, see how well loved you are; that is because a filial child is always loved."

Fay went over and put the red jacket against Lin. The red was lovely against her black hair and the blouse seemed to be a perfect fit. Fay said, "She can wear it now; it seems to be just the right size."

Sun said, "Fook should have ordered it made a little larger; she will not get enough wear out of it."

Grandfather Kwong said, "Let us see about the pink one."

The pink one, ordered by Grandmother Kwong, was as yet too large to wear. Grandfather Kwong said, "Next year, next year . . . you can wear this next year. This color brings out the pink in Lin; do you all notice?"

All agreed, even young Kiang.

Grandfather Kwong said, "Sun, read the letter now."

Sun had wanted to read it alone in his small office before having to read it out loud to everyone. But in this conservative family filial obedience was expected from all; from a grown son to his elderly father, from a grown brother to his older brother, and most certainly from young children to all above them.

Sun reached into a pocket for the letter from Fook that had arrived in the mail early that morning. He read it in a monotone, pausing occasionally to clear his throat. All listened with attention, Grandfather Kwong's eyes toward the floor, his head nodding at certain points of the letter.

In the letter Fook wrote that the ocean voyage had been pleasant and without particular incident. The peach and plum blossoms were in unusual beauty and abundance this year. He had taken his wife and children to Hong Kong and Canton, and next week they expected to spend several days in Macao. Grandmother Kwong was in good health and anxiously awaiting the day when she would see Lin and Kiang for the first time. His search among the shops in Canton and Hong Kong had proved fruitful and he was returning to San Francisco with many rare pieces of art.

The next part of the letter was directed at Lin and Kiang. The red costume, Fook wrote, was a duplicate of one his own daughter Ying had. He thought it so charming that he had ordered one for Lin; the seamstress in Canton was nearly eighty years old, yet had finished the outfit in three days. His daughter Ying could write beautiful characters and she was studying under a teacher who was a happy combination of the old and the new. If Lin and Kiang were back in the House that Tai Ming Built,

they too would be writing beautiful characters and reading bits of Confucius as well as Chinese history. He was
bringing Kiang three large kites; a carp, an eagle and a
dragon, all with eyes that moved.

Also, wrote Fook, he was bringing back some samples
of preserved fruits for Grandfather Kwong and Sun's approval. Fook thought they were of excellent quality and
might be imported. He had also gone to their porcelain
dealer and had been promised credit for the rice bowls
that had been chipped because of overcrowding in the
shipping crates.

A postscript was inserted, saying that an old photograph of Tai Ming was enclosed; he had come across it
folded in a book. When, wondered Fook, was this picture
taken of Tai Ming in front of his store, his two feet stiff
upon the sidewalk of San Francisco?

Fook wrote that he had read and reread the blue-
bound book of Tai Ming and his trip to California but
regrettably it ended with Tai Ming's return to the Hills
of Tong after his three years' search for gold. Certainly
what followed was of interest too, and had he, Fook, the
talent he would take up brush and ink to stroke down the
story that followed, but unfortunately, though the incli-
nation was there, the ability was absent.

A simultaneous sigh rose from everyone after the letter
was read. Lin's hand was waving in the air as she cried
out, "Father, Father, look for the picture!" Sun looked into
the long, narrow envelope, then tapped its corner on the
counter and turned it upside down. A small photograph
slid out.

The picture showed Tai Ming in his mature years; a
man not tall, but well proportioned, a man whose head
was big, whose ears were large and heavy, whose mouth was

also large; all, according to the village geomancer, signs of a successful and prosperous man. The picture showed how his eyes looked straight forward as they always did, for his heart was upright.

A smile broke over Grandfather Kwong's face as he looked at the picture, the smile gradually broadening as each detail he examined brought back memories of days in earlier San Francisco. He remembered the horse-drawn vehicles, the odor from the gas lamps, the high, narrow windows of the houses and shops, and most of all Grandfather Kwong remembered his industrious grandfather, old Tai Ming.

Indeed Tai Ming was industrious, young Tai Ming, now for almost two years returned from California. He did not then know it, dressed as he was in long satin robes, eating and drinking the best served from the hands of servants in his magnificent house built with gold from the mountains of California. He knew only that he was restless, not suspecting that after two years of leisure and luxury he was already satiated. As he slept after a day's holiday in the teahouses of Canton, he suddenly began to think of California. His thoughts of the place and its people were kind now, and he had forgotten how bitter his feelings had been when he sailed from San Francisco Bay back to the Hills of Tong. Time had healed all his wounds, those of his body and those of his heart. Then he began to yearn for the days when he had dug and sweated, when he fell asleep exhausted to awake the next day fresh and eager, when his heart leaped at the sight of an ounce of gold, steady and heavy under a trembling pool of water in a metal pan.

But his mother could not understand his decision to leave again for California and adamantly asserted that a wife and many sons would cure him of his restlessness. But for the first and only time in his life Tai Ming was unfilial and obstinately maintained his intention to leave. In the end his mother reluctantly consented.

But his uncle Ming Wah understood and with pomposity quoted a proverb, "Unequivocally men ought not to be one day without employment, for surely as excessive wine breeds inferior men so daily idleness breeds foul corruption!"

So once again Tai Ming sailed to California. But in San Francisco, many of his countrymen told him that life for the man with the queue in the mining country was still unpleasant. Gold was getting scarce, and the white men were now building dams to divert the mountain streams into wooden flumes and thus dig in the stream bed itself. There was little left for Tai Ming to work. Tai Ming agreed; it would be unwise to return to gold mining. Instead he decided to become a merchant in town.

The first Tai Ming Company was a small shop and its shelves and counters were put up by Tai Ming himself. His uncle Ming Wah was his supplier and periodically Tai Ming rented a horse-drawn wagon to drive down to the wharf to get his shipments of sweet ginger, coconut strips and dried preserved fruits.

Six months later the store burned to the ground. The second Tai Ming Company was larger than the first and was located a block away from where the original had stood. A large silk tapestry with fringes on its hem, brilliant with gold symbols of good luck, hung on the front wall. It was a gift from his uncle Ming Wah, on receiving word that the first store had burned after only six months.

Immediately Ming Wah had shipped the gift to Tai Ming, so that prosperity and good luck would always linger within the four walls of the Tai Ming Company.

The tapestry served the Tai Ming Company well. The store, like the City, gradually outgrew its awkwardness and crudeness. Against the background of the red-and-gold tapestry stood fine wares of pewter, porcelain, cinnabar, cloisonné, ivory and brass. Ming Wah had written, "The red tapestry will foster prosperity and protection forever!" Prosperity rained upon the Tai Ming Company, and protection for almost half a century, not forever, for the red tapestry and the Tai Ming Company burned to the ground along with almost all of San Francisco in the great fire and earthquake of 1906.

When the second Tai Ming Company was a year old, Tai Ming received a most important letter from his uncle Ming Wah. In this letter he was advised to return home as soon as possible, for a wife had been selected for him. His horoscope and the horoscope of the girl had been exchanged and everything had been found to be in harmony. To this Tai Ming wholeheartedly agreed. It was time for him to take a wife. He was a successful merchant now and surely he would need sons to help him and take over the business when he was old. Leaving the store in charge of a trusted clerk, Tai Ming returned home to his village. As with all matches of those times, he did not see his bride until the marriage ceremonies. His bride was dainty and lovely, her skin as smooth as the white of an egg, and her most skillfully bound, tiny feet measured only three inches.

Tai Ming stayed in his village home for three months. When he was certain that his wife was with child, he returned to his business in San Francisco. As was the pattern in those days of the Chinese emigrant, his wife stayed behind. Months later he received the joyous news that a son had been born and that many relatives and friends were expected to be received at the house for the child's full-month celebration.

Tai Ming saw his son for the first time when the child was over a year old, when once again he returned to his village home. Several months later he again left for San Francisco, leaving behind his son and his wife who was again with child.

He did not see any of his children until they were a year old, at which time he returned to the village home. In time Tai Ming was the father of two sons and three daughters who saw him once a year for two or three months. When Tai Ming's sons reached the ages of fourteen and fifteen respectively, they came to San Francisco at his written request. Thereafter, Tai Ming made no more trips back to his village until he retired from the business at the age of sixty-one.

Both sons had much of Tai Ming's industrious spirit. Day into night they clerked in the store in San Francisco. In time they too were summoned by letter to return home, each to take the wife selected for him. As was the proper custom, the elder son left first and a year later the second son left. As in the case of Tai Ming, the wives stayed behind, seeing their husbands once a year for a period of two or three months.

Tai Ming was blessed with many grandsons and granddaughters. In time, his oldest grandson came to San Francisco, this oldest grandson being Grandfather Kwong, grandfather of Lin and Kiang. Several years later, Grandfather Kwong, a young man then, returned to China to take the bride selected for him by the women in the family.

When Tai Ming reached the age of sixty-one, several years before the end of the nineteenth century, he was feted on his birthday with a huge banquet in a restaurant on old Dupont Street. Courses and courses of fine food were served. Last to be served were bowls of noodles, symbolizing long life. Each guest was presented with a red porcelain rice bowl and a pair of ivory chopsticks as a wish that he would also have the good fortune to celebrate his sixty-first birthday. It was a dual celebration, for Tai Ming was also ready to retire from business. He was soon to return home, home being, of course, the Hills of Tong—China.

Tai Ming returned home, young and restless no more, at last feeling he was entitled to leisure and comfort. It was then that he built the garden adjacent to his house, the garden with the peach and plum trees, set against the delicate blades of heavenly bamboos.

Though Tai Ming was of humble origin, in his retirement, he began to read the words of Confucius and Mencius. Daily, in the small octagonal pavilion on the hill, he held a soft-bound book in his old hands and read from noon to dusk, pausing often to look at the garden he grew to love so much.

As predicted long ago by the local geomancer, Tai Ming lived to a very old age. "If the space behind the ears will not permit a finger, the age of eighty will be passed," the geomancer had told Tai Ming, and true to the forecast he lived until the age of eighty-seven. Though his body was frail, his mind was alert and on his last day on earth, with the help of two grandsons, he walked through his garden. He died in the evening. Toward the end his words were that all his male descendants must return home to China, wherever they might spend their youth; that they must be industrious when young, whether at home or abroad, but in their late years they must meditate and study in the garden with the camelback bridge.

For the last few minutes of Tai Ming's life he was back in the gold-mining country of California. His dark eyes were suddenly bright, his thin, outstretched hands trembled excitedly as he shouted "Gold!" and Tai Ming was dead at the venerable age of eighty-seven.

All the male descendants of Tai Ming adhered faithfully to his last request. Some went abroad to the Tai Ming Company in San Francisco; others branched out to Singapore, some to Manila. Others stayed in China to cultivate the farms, collect rents, and invest in real estate in Canton. Wherever they went, they were one day summoned by an important letter to return home to take the bride chosen for them. Then, no matter how long they had worked and lived abroad, eventually they returned to the Hills of Tong, to the magnificent home that later came to be known as the House that Tai Ming Built.

THE DINING TABLE IN THE KITCHEN WAS SET FOR A SPECIAL occasion. For Grandfather Kwong's last dinner in San Francisco, a new red oilcloth was spread upon the large round table in the center of the room.

Tonight the family was to eat from blue-and-white bowls with the incised rice grain pattern and partake of soup from matching spoons. Ivory chopsticks in place of the usual wooden ones had been placed alongside the bowls.

Fay set a tureen of steaming hot, rich, bird's-nest soup on the table. She had worked all day preparing the food and now the family eyed the dishes with appreciation, Grandfather Kwong extolling her culinary talents. "Bird's-nest soup, squids with greens, deep fried squabs, braised mushrooms, steamed chicken; this is indeed a fine dinner!"

Fay busied herself filling everyone's rice bowl, pretending she had not heard Grandfather Kwong's compliment. Always there existed a small degree of formality between Fay and Grandfather Kwong. Courtesy was always accorded

[59]

each other, familiarities never exchanged. He never attempted to influence her in any way for it was not within his province to do so, yet she would never do anything in his presence that would not meet with his approval. Were Fay in the House that Tai Ming Built, however, she would be dominated by Grandmother Kwong, though it was a most subtle kind of domination.

The family had been feted with farewell dinners by distant relatives and friends all the preceding week. This last evening was a dinner at home just for the family.

All were seated in their chairs. Grandfather Kwong looked briefly at Fay. His thoughts were: she was a good daughter-in-law, a fine mother; it was unfortunate that her health was such that only two children were born of the marriage, but then were not these things determined by fate?

Sun looked at Grandfather Kwong, thinking it would be strange not to see his father about anymore. This day had always been expected but it had come so soon, as quickly as the blinking of an eye. Now Sun looked at his daughter Lin and his son Kiang, one on each side of Grandfather Kwong. While Kiang playfully rubbed his stomach and licked his mouth as he eyed the food, Lin leaned against Grandfather Kwong's shoulder, her little face sad. The child had been disappointed so many times; perhaps in another six months Fay would be well enough and she and the children could sail for China. Secretly Sun was happy they were still with him and had been able to stay so long; this was a secret he had not even confided to his wife. On the contrary, each time Fay and the children's trip had been postponed he had written without delay to the House that Tai Ming Built, offering profuse apologies, explaining in minute detail the reasons for postponement, and how excellent the reasons had been.

Fay concentrated on the bird's-nest soup, eating very little food and rice. Her appetite was still not quite normal, her strength not yet what it used to be. She would miss Grandfather Kwong for she was exceedingly fond of her father-in-law. But then what woman could not help but be fond of someone who loved her children so; she had always been especially touched by his attentions to Lin, unusual in a family steeped in the traditional belief that sons and many sons must be born to carry on the family name, and while daughters are loved, they belong to another family once they are married off.

"A little herb brandy?" asked Sun of Grandfather Kwong.

'A tiny bit, just a tiny bit, Sun," replied Grandfather Kwong, extending him a small wine cup to be filled.

Sun did not drink and Grandfather Kwong said, "That will be all. Kiang, take the wine and set it back in the cupboard."

Had Fook been present, the pottery jug of wine would have been placed near him to be totally consumed with the dinner. The round-faced Fook liked a sip of wine with each bite of meat and by the end of a meal he would be twice as merry and loud as his usual merry self. Fook was to have been back in San Francisco last month but his son had suddenly been taken very ill and he had stayed on in the House that Tai Ming Built. His son had recovered, but Fook had decided to stay a little longer so that he could spend some time with Grandfather Kwong when the latter arrived in China.

"Mui Mui, take some of the soup. It has cooked all

day and it is beneficial to your body," said Grandfather Kwong to Lin who had hardly eaten. The pieces of chicken and greens he had picked up for her remained in her rice bowl untouched.

The child sighed. She looked at Grandfather Kwong and said, her voice trembling a little: "How can I eat when I'm so sad. Tomorrow you will be gone and I shall never see you again."

Grandfather Kwong put his bowl and chopsticks down and took her hands. He said, "But we shall meet again. You, your mother and Elder Brother are sailing in another month or so to join me."

"Yes, but always something happens and we cannot go," said the child.

Grandfather Kwong turned his face away and stared into space. He said seriously, "Ah, such is fate." Sun and Fay nodded their heads in agreement, for they too believed that everything was decreed by fate. But in another moment Grandfather Kwong was serious no more and he said to Lin, "Mui Mui, the day before you sail, your father will write me a letter. I shall calculate on which day you will arrive and I shall have tea and melon seeds ready in the pavilion in the garden. Perhaps by then the lotuses will be in full bloom and together we will view them as we sit and drink fragrant tea." And not to neglect Kiang, Grandfather Kwong said to him: "The weather may still be right to sail kites for one who is so full of energy he cannot sit still."

"Goldfish in the garden pool, a camelback bridge to climb, a peony-shaped door to go in and out—I shall see them yet!" exclaimed Lin, her faith restored that she would eventually see the House that Tai Ming Built. Her appetite returned and she ate quickly, making each piece of food disappear as soon as it was deposited on her bowl by Grandfather Kwong.

Dinner was over. Tonight tea was being served in the kitchen rather than taken leisurely in the living room as was usual. All were expected to retire early. They would have to get up early the next morning to see Grandfather Kwong off to the Hills of Tong.

Sun led the way up the gangplank, Grandfather Kwong's suitcase in one hand. Fay followed with Kiang occasionally jerking the hand of her excited son to hurry him along. Trailing far behind were Grandfather Kwong and Lin, both walking slowly, for he was not young and she was very small. Sun reached the deck and waited for the rest of the family. He was more serious than ever, standing straight and slim in his good, dark suit, his head lifted upward because of his high stiff collar. Now came Fay, her face pale in the daylight, the high neckline of her blue Chinese dress showing above the collar of her western-style coat, pulling Kiang, dressed in a tight jacket and pants, a sporty cap upon his head. Laughter followed along with Lin and Grandfather Kwong, he pretending he was being pulled by her, hearing and not minding one bit that she unfilially called him a slow turtle. They went in search of Grandfather Kwong's private stateroom and found it to be comfortable and attractive. At once Lin and Kiang began roaming about. Fay alternated between a frown on her face as she watched the children, and brief wistful smiles directed at Grandfather Kwong, as if in deep regret that she was not also sailing to China.

Sun and Grandfather Kwong were now carrying on a serious last-minute talk, the latter wearing a dark, padded gown, now that he was leaving the West forever. Sun nodded his head in agreement with each point Grandfather Kwong made, talking with one hand slowing waving in the air, as he always did when the subject matter was serious.

"Sun, let me remind you once again of the two loans owing us: Mr. Hong the herbalist, and Mr. Lee the grocer. These were loans made through me and I have collected through the years, but they, of course, know that now the matter is in your hands. Now if, after the tenth of the month, a payment has not been brought in to you, don't hesitate to call upon them for the money. It will not offend them; more than likely they were too busy to go to you; the money is always there. Sun—another matter yet—ah, ah, ah, what do we have here. . . ."

Two small, warm hands softly folded Grandfather Kwong's hand and his face turned to meet Lin's staring up at him in wide-eyed sadness. She wore a long red woolen scarf on her head tied at the neck and the freshly trimmed fringe of hair across her forehead was straight and even. Her best red woolen coat was inches below her knees, and her long red woolen stockings met the hemline of the coat.

"Mui Mui, Mui Mui! Do you think I have forgotten you?"

"Have you? I waited so long while you talked."

Grandfather Kwong bent down to Lin. "Indeed I have not forgotten you, not for a moment. I must be very old and very foolish to waste precious last moments to talk of loans and such when I could be spending them with you and Elder Brother. Come—Kiang too—take my hand and climb up on the seat and look out of the window."

Lin and Kiang looked out of the round porthole.

"For days and days I will be sailing these waters. Then in a week's time I shall see the Hills of Tong."

Lin turned her head to face him. She said, "I shall miss you; indeed I shall," she said with great tenderness.

Grandfather Kwong looked at her gently and said nothing. He had put the question to Fay whether it would be agreeable if Lin and Kiang were to leave with him, and for Fay to sail when she was stronger. Fay had been most hesitant in her reply, and really it had not been necessary for her to answer; it had been in her eyes. With three miscarriages close to each other, undoubtedly she could never have another child; how then could anyone have the right to ask her to part with her children, even for a little while?

Lin pulled Grandfather Kwong's hand and said again, now emphatically as if she had thought over her original statement and was now confirming it: "Yes, I shall miss you."

Still Grandfather Kwong said nothing for he felt if he were to tell her that his pain in leaving her was as great as hers, there would be no end to her unhappiness. Instead he sat down on the seat, gathered her in his arms, and reaching into his pocket, produced a farewell present of a dollar bill wrapped in red paper and a bag of her favorite ginger. Instantly she was in tears with her face against his coat, wondering in her childishly selfish mind who was ever going to buy her red ginger again.

The signal sounded for all visitors to leave the ship. Grandfather Kwong's head darted upward and a smile was on his face. For a brief moment he was back in the House that Tai Ming Built. In another second the smile was gone, for now the ship was soon to cast off and he was to see no more of his son and his family. He would not see Sun, for many years to come; in that moment of departure his daughter-in-law Fay looked pale and fragile and he was deeply concerned; his grandson Kiang he would miss and the companionship of his beloved Lin he would surely miss the most. The thought flashed through him that he need not sail. Then the signal sounded again and in a gesture spontaneous and rare, he embraced Sun, Fay, Lin and Kiang, who only now, at the very last moment, burst into tears.

Slowly the family walked down the gangplank to the pier to wave Grandfather Kwong farewell. It was windier now than it had been earlier and they saw the hem of Grandfather Kwong's long gown flapping against his trousers as he stood on deck. The blare of the ship's horn sounded, and the propeller thrashed the water. Suddenly a desperate longing for Grandfather Kwong seized Lin and she ran off from the family. She stopped a few yards ahead and standing with legs apart and arms outstretched, she cried: "Take me with you to the Hills of Tong!" But all was in vain, for the ship was already far off and Lin and Grandfather Kwong were never to meet again.

Part Two

A Fragrance of

Sandalwood

"Opium! Opium! as good as the immortal's pill; puff it but once and it is equal to entering heaven. . . ."

Grandfather Kwong was back in the Hills of Tong and the little girl who had so desperately wanted to go with him to the House that Tai Ming Built had found a new companion. The words he had feebly uttered were meant as a farewell.

"Tomorrow I will come back again. May I come or may I not come?" Lin inquired of her elderly friend, who lay dreamily in the wooden bunk that occupied half of his small dingy room. Floating in heaven, he merely waved a thin yellow hand and nodded his shrunken head in consent. Lin dashed down the shaky, odorous, dark stairs, for the stories of demons and spirits which her old friend had told her were still fresh in her young head.

". . . and at the hour of the rat, the dogs howled and sleeping children suddenly screamed, for the eyes of dogs and children saw the evil spirit that we grown people only felt. . . ."

[69]

It was the next afternoon and, bearing a bag of fruit in her arms which she had taken in secret from home, Lin was once again with her old opium-smoking friend. ". . . It was the soul of a man who had died a violent death. He had returned to our village, wandering all about to find and steal a body, to reanimate it and continue to live. That night, huddled in my bed I felt the cold of a shaky form bend over and blow out the candle on the table near my bed I had left burning in fear of the dark. Then later the icy hand of the demon stroked my face, but right at that moment the village watchman on his route struck his gong and instantly the demon disappeared. Early the next morning I took hammer and nails and built a wooden screen behind my door so that if the demon tried to enter my house again he would bump his head and become confused. Then I changed the pathway leading to my door, for demons travel in a straight line and in this way the evil spirit would be frustrated."

"Ah . . ." Lin sighed, knowing she surely would have a nightmare again that night.

"One morning in our village we found the body of a young farmer on the ground. His throat had been chewed to pieces. And do you know why? For years the woman he was married to had not been a woman but a were-tiger who had assumed the shape of a beautiful woman."

Lin, her coat draping her head and huddled shoulders, asked, "But how did you know it was a were-tiger?"

"Ah, Little One, all of us in the village searched for the dead man's wife, but in vain. Then we remembered how peculiar it was that such a beautiful woman had always shunned a mirror or a pool of water that might show her reflection; for you see, Little One, although a were-tiger has assumed the shape of a human, his true image is always reflected in a mirror."

Lin's friend climbed laboriously out of his wooden bunk and slowly walked to a kitchen table to pour two cups of tea. "Little One, enough of were-animals and evil spirits. Sit and partake of some tea. Ah . . . with a good companion and a cup of tea, one is equal to the immortals."

She liked the words and she repeated them, not understanding their meaning: "With a good companion and a cup of tea, one is equal to the immortals."

Her old friend's sharp black teeth clicked noisily together in joy at her appreciation of his words. His watery brown eyes were merry for a second and he said in his feeble, trembling voice: "Little One, you like the proverbs? Ah, I know many more. Though I am but an old man now living in a shabby room, once I taught school in our village. Listen, Little One, I shall quote you more proverbs."

They sat facing each other on wooden stools, their elbows on the top of a stained red oilcloth covering a table littered with soft-bound books and stale food. Her friend sucked a slice of orange and Lin sucked a slice of orange. He took a sip of tea and she took a sip of tea. He began in his feeble, trembling voice, "The wise are happiest near water; the virtuous are happiest near hills."

She repeated it in his jingling fashion, stressing and prolonging the tones of the last word like the final upward stroke of a word character. " 'The wise are happiest near water; the virtuous are happiest near hills.' Why, sir?"

His watery eyes twinkled for a second, and with a finger he wiped a teardrop away from his gaunt cheekbone.

"Because, Little One, the wise are active and restless like the waters; the virtuous are tranquil and firm like the solid mountains."

A sip of tea and a slice of orange again, and the wavering voice went on: "If you would enlarge your fields of happiness, you must level the soil in your heart." And like a proud teacher he pursed his withered mouth as Lin repeated the words she liked but did not understand.

"Little One, it means one must be honest and steady in all that one does."

One bony yellow finger poised in the air, eyes solemn, Lin's friend softly chanted, "He who tells me of my weakness is my teacher; he who tells me of my virtues, does me harm." Then his finger tapped in rhythm to the words repeated out of her young mouth.

Then in a lively tempo he quoted one proverb after another, and just as rapidly Lin repeated each one. Though she was but six, her memory was precocious.

"As riches adorn the house, so virtue adorns the man."

"Return injury with justice, and return kindness with kindness."

"Be not distressed that men do not know you; be distressed that you do not know men."

The tempo became livelier still as he chanted and she repeated, "The superior man seeks to perfect the best in men; the mean man seeks to perfect the worst in men.

"The superior man is easy to serve and hard to please; the mean man is hard to serve and easy to please."

Suddenly the flapping sounds of wings beat against the little window directly above the bunk bed. Lin turned her head. A small gray pigeon perched on the window ledge, peeking in at them with wide-open eyes. Her old friend raised his head toward the window. He was not happy at the sight of the bird. With a bony hand and in a voice as loud as he could muster, he warned the pigeon, "Away! Away!"

The little pigeon tried to squeeze himself through the narrow slit of the opened window. Feverishly excited, his hands trembling, eyes rolling and lips quivering, Lin's old friend pressed a shaky hand on her shoulder to raise himself from his chair. Shoulders stooped, bony knees bent, toes pointed outward, he hopped on his worn slippers, his eyes every second on the pigeon. His thin hands clutched the soiled quilt and with an effort he pulled himself up onto the bed. There he rested for a second in a kneeling position, then heaved a sigh, and stood up. Like a stern teacher of the old Confucian school, he pointed a warning finger at the pigeon, then pushed its beak away from the window. Finally, with a last convulsive effort, he shut the window, a highly visible cloud of dust mushrooming forth with the noise of the slam.

Solemnly, still standing on the bunk bed he intoned, "If into your house flies the wild bird, misfortune will follow, mark my word!"

He remained standing on the bed until he was certain the pigeon had flown away. Again, with much effort, he proceeded to come down. Standing close to Lin, he slapped his hands to get rid of the dust. Then with his head cocked, his withered mouth pursed, one hand on his hip, one finger on his forehead, he pondered upon the wisdom of what he had done as he said, "Perhaps I should have fried it for my supper."

He sat down. He said: "Little One, let us go on with the proverbs. Listen—the superior man is ruled by propriety; the mean man is ruled by law. The superior man thinks of righteousness; the mean man thinks of profit."

The sight of his hair in disarray disturbed Lin. The wind from the open window had blown it in all directions. Its disorder distracted her and caused her to stumble as she repeated the proverbs.

She said: "Sir, your hair is quite disordered. If you would give me a comb, I'll arrange your hair for you."

He said, "Little One, I don't have a comb." He lifted a thin hand to his mouth, moistened the palm generously, then put it to his head to slick his hair back to her satisfaction.

Lin's old friend laughed softly.

She asked, "What is so funny, sir?"

He said, "Little One, I don't have a comb, is that not unfortunate? Shall we then proceed to the Buddhist Temple of our village to acquire one?"

She loved make-believe. She replied, "Yes, let's leave right now!"

Lin's old friend laughed in his weak, wavering voice. He said: "Little One! I have fooled you completely! Don't you know the favorite joke of us Sons of Tong? Little One, remember always that Buddhist monks shave their heads and a Buddhist temple would be the least likely place to find a comb!"

Lin bounced up and down in her chair with laughter; surely Elder Brother would not be able to tell a more clever joke tonight at the evening rice!

A light rap on the table for silence and the wavering voice again:

"The superior man is satisfied and serene; the mean man is forever in anxiety.

"The superior man considers sincerity the most excellent of all virtues.

"The superior man is stern at a distance; mild up close; firm and clear in conversation."

Simultaneously they heaved deep sighs, rang out in joyous laughter, and sipped cool tea from chipped porcelain cups.

Lin's old friend spoke with deep conviction, "Little One, you are indeed a clever child!"

Said Lin with equal conviction, "Sir, you are indeed good of heart to say so!"

Said he, with palms outstretched, "Little One, we are so well acquainted; why then do you address me Sir this, Sir that?"

Said she, with palms outstretched: "Sir, it is always my mother who teaches me how to address my elders and she is not here. How then do you wish me to address you, for I am most desirous of pleasing you?"

Her old friend chuckled softly. He said in his feeble voice: "So clever indeed! Little One, address me as Uncle, that would be appropriate."

She nodded her small head in approval. She said: "Yes, Uncle. Uncle, partake of some hot tea," and with a pair of unsteady small hands she poured tea for him out of a brown earthen teapot.

He began again, his hand holding one old ivory chopstick which he pointed in the air, "The superior man stands in awe of the laws of Heaven; he stands in awe of all great men; he stands in awe of the wise words of the sages."

She commenced to repeat the words but with a bony hand he silenced her as he continued, "The mean man, not knowing the laws of Heaven, does not stand in awe of them; not understanding great men, does not respect them; not believing the words of wisdom, disparages them."

Preferring the superior man to the mean man, she repeated, " 'The superior man stands in awe of the laws of Heaven; he stands in awe of all great men; he stands in awe of the wise words of the sages.' "

"How clever indeed! A mind as good as the sages indeed! Let us see how clever you can be with this one. Listen: 'The superior man is anxious that his eyes see clearly; anxious that his ears hear distinctly; anxious that his appearance be benevolent; anxious that his conduct be respectful; anxious that his speech be sincere; anxious that in business he is ethical; anxious when in doubt to question; anxious about difficulties when aroused; anxious about righteousness when tempted."

She drew a deep breath and recited rapidly, but half-way through she became confused and hung her head in shame.

"Ah, Little One, do not fret. Here, allow me to give you these books of proverbs. When you are a grown girl you can read for yourself and learn."

Emulating the ways of her elders she refused, but he insisted. Then, after the lapse of a proper interval, she accepted the books with words of deepest gratitude. She hugged the books to her young breast and listened to her old friend.

"The superior man is anxious lest he should not get truth; he is not anxious that poverty is his lot."

His benevolence overwhelmed her young person and seeing his shrunken, kind face she remembered Grandfather Kwong, and her heart quickened with fear. Placing a small hand over his small bony hand, she asked, "Will you return to the Hills of Tong someday?"

He said, "Ah, to return to the Hills of Tong—that

would be good. But, Little One, I have not the funds to return."

At this, in secret she was happy.

Lin's old friend got up from the wooden stool and walked over to a table near his bunk. Quietly she walked over and joined him and watched carefully as he took a small ivory stick to pick up a blob of opium from a tin. Then he held the stick over a gas jet flame, turning and turning it until the opium formed into a little round ball. Next he put the little ball of opium into the bowl of a long, slender pipe which he held in his bony hands with tender care. It was Lin's cue that she should make ready to leave. Very softly she walked out of the room after he uttered the words, "Opium, opium, as good as the immortal's pill. . . ."

"In autumn the trees shed their leaves; in spring they blossom again, but the cruelty of Heaven is that when a man grows old he cannot grow young again!"

Lin's old friend was unhappy as he talked and Lin, with a gift of a single orange in her hand, was also unhappy. There were present in the room two white men and she was concerned, for one orange would not be enough for the four of them.

"Uncle, what is the trouble? In all the many moons I have been to see you, I have never seen you like this."

He said: "Heaven has a path, but I did not tread it; hell has no door, but I charged into it. Little One, there can no longer be any more happy hours with us. Now you must learn the proverbs yourself. I have taught you the characters and you are clever; you will learn."

Her heart quickened. She said, "I do not understand! I do not understand! Why can there no longer be happy hours with us?"

His bony hands waved weakly in the air. "These two foreigners are going to take me somewhere for a few days. Then afterward I am returning to the Hills of Tong."

And although it had been almost a year since he had told her, she remembered and she cried out: "Uncle, you told me you had not the funds to return to the Hills of Tong!"

In sympathy he handed her a dirty handkerchief and she wiped the tears from her young eyes. Patting her small hands he said: "I am truly sorry; but, Little One, these two foreigners insist I return and since they are so kind as to pay my passage fare, I must not offend them. Little One, is that not the way of the superior man?"

She nodded her unhappy head and replied in a choking voice, now fully understanding the words, "Yes—the superior man subdues himself; the mean man is resentful and domineering."

Lin's old friend walked slowly out of the room between the two white men. She stayed behind: there would be no more proverbs, no more stories of were-tigers and evil spirits, no more enchanting fables of the Eight Immortals. She ran out of the dingy room and, standing with legs apart and arms outstretched, she cried, as she had cried to Grandfather Kwong, "Uncle, take me with you to the Hills of Tong." But he did not hear her and with his soiled handkerchief pressed to her sobbing mouth, she watched him disappear.

Years later she came upon the old books her opium-addict friend had given her. Opening them, she remembered his feeble, trembling voice, his withered finger poised in the air as he quoted: "He who tells me of my weakness is my teacher; he who tells me of my virtues does me harm." Putting the books aside, she knew then what as a little heartbroken girl she did not know: That last day her old friend had been taken away by narcotics agents to be deported back to the Hills of Tong.

THE COLLAR OF SUN'S BLACK COAT WAS TURNED UP AND his hands were in his pockets. It was July in San Francisco, and the weather was damp and cold on Pier 46. His gaze was directed upward at the gangplank, his eyes serious, his chin and mouth firm. A steady stream of happy people walked down the gangplank, shouting greetings to friends and relatives below. At the distance where he stood from the liner, Sun had already mistaken several short, moon-round Sons of Tong for Fook, and each time his hand had gone up in the air in greeting. Not wishing to repeat his mistake, he now squinted his eyes to see better, determined to avoid any further foolish gesture.

At last he saw F   There could be no mistake about it this time; this wa Fook with his moon-round face and his rotund body. Sun's face broke out in a broad smile, and one slim hand waved energetically to his brother, home at last from the House that Tai Ming Built. From the deck, Fook did not see Sun but his eyes searched for him. As usual, Fook was in high spirits, his round face lit up with good will. When at last he saw Sun his eyes and hand darted up simultaneously with a cry of "Ah!" and his applelike head nodded rhythmically to tell Sun that he would soon be below.

Fook walked swiftly up to Sun and because they were both so genuinely happy to see each other they met in a spontaneous embrace.

"Elder Brother! Elder Brother! So good to see you!" cried Fook loudly.

"Fook! Fook! It is good to have you back!"

They were a conservative family; Fook had called Sun Elder Brother since the former was able to talk and would continue to do so no matter what his age, but Sun had the right to call Fook by his first name.

"Ah! And how are Sister-in-Law, Kiang and Lin?"

"The danger is over for Lin now. We were very worried about her hearing when complications set in with the measles! She wanted very badly to come to meet you."

"How very touching," said Fook.

Sun's face was kindly now, not serious. He said, "You have been gone almost a year."

"Almost—almost—Elder Brother. Consequently, I shall not make the trip next year."

"Has it been agreed upon?"

"Yes, the matter was settled."

"Fook, you must tell me all that happened at home."

"Assuredly! Pictures! I have so many, many pictures to show you!"

"Fook, let's find a taxicab."

Fook's arm went up to touch Sun's shoulder as they walked in search of a taxi. Once again they were opposites. Sun had assumed his serious look while Fook was his usual cheerful self. Fook dropped his arm from Sun's shoulder. His brother was a full head taller than he, and with his other hand holding a suitcase, he had begun to get tired.

Fook looked at his brother, understanding the serious look on Sun's face, knowing Sun for a man thoroughly honest and upright, but too serious and, alas, quite literal-minded. The two brothers were exceedingly fond of each other and unquestioningly loyal. Theirs was a relationship completely void of jealousy or envy in matters small or large.

Sun and Fook were native-born Californians, as were another brother and two sisters. They had sailed to the Hills of Tong when the youngest child was able to walk, going with their mother while their father remained in San Francisco. Back in the House that Tai Ming Built, they had been taught by private tutors, continuing on to private schools, and finishing their education in a university in Canton. Then Sun and Fook had left China to return to the Tai Ming Company to help their father, Grandfather Kwong, grandfather of Lin and Kiang.

A few years later, because tradition decreed that the oldest son should be the first to take a wife, Sun was summoned by letter to return home to China to take the bride selected for him. That had been Fay, and Sun had taken her back to San Francisco with him.

Fook was summoned home next to take the bride selected for him. Like Tai Ming, Fook had left his wife in China, making annual visits abroad to his family, now composed of four sons and one daughter.

The brothers sat back comfortably in the taxi. Fook took out an envelope filled with pictures of the family to show Sun.

"The third son bears a strong resemblance to Kiang, don't you think?"

"A handsome boy, indeed. This one resembles Cousin Poy, don't you think? Cousin Poy who is now in Singapore, but then it has been years since I've seen Cousin Poy," said Sun.

"This is daughter Ying! The same age as Lin and as quick and intelligent as Lin but with none of Lin's delicate beauty. Unfortunately she has inherited my frame and face and she is inches shorter than Lin."

"Ah—she is charming!" said Sun.

"She is very sweet. Perhaps the blame is not altogether mine that she is round and short. Her mother gets fatter each year I see her. It will be another two years before I see my wife again and I shudder to think how she will look then!"

Fook chuckled softly. Sun raised his eyebrows, slightly dismayed that his brother should speak so of his wife. He himself would never have made such a remark, but then Fay was as slender as the day when he first saw her, the day of their wedding.

Sun said softly, "Fook, you should not talk like that."

Fook laughed good-naturedly, "Joking! I was merely joking! She is a good woman!"

Sun resumed his study of the pictures. "Ah, a picture of Father sitting in the garden."

Fook took the picture of Grandfather Kwong from Sun's hand. He held it at arm's length. "Yes, a picture to Lin from Father. This is how he spends much of his days; dressed in a long gown, a cup of tea beside him, a volume in front of him, and fragrant leaves all about him as he sits in the pavilion upon the hill. He wrote a verse for Lin on the back of this picture. Let me read it to you:

" 'In the pavilion upon the hill,
My heart with pleasure it is filled;
But my Mui Mui she is not here,
So my pleasure is mingled with tears.' "

The two brothers laughed softly together at Grandfather Kwong's verse. Fook said, "He concludes with this sentence to Lin: 'I hope that as of this writing you yourself are able to read the words of my very poor verse.' "

Fook chuckled again. Sun's brows knitted together. He said: "Unfortunately the teacher who promised to start their lessons has taken a position elsewhere and neither Kiang nor Lin has begun their Chinese. It will be disturbing to Father to know that they cannot read yet." He shook his head.

Fook chuckled again, slightly louder now. Sun looked at him in an attempt to understand the laughter. Fook averted his face from his brother's. He dared not tell Sun that he was laughing at him.

They arrived in front of the Tai Ming Company to be greeted by Mr. Lum, a young employee, who was cleaning the window with a feather duster. Profuse and loud greetings were exchanged between Fook and Mr. Lum, and repeated with the other employee in the store. Fook and Sun entered the house through the back door of the Tai Ming Company.

Fay had been waiting, and now she greeted Fook cordially, addressing him as her children did. "Second Uncle, you are back. You must have a cup of tea."

"Sister-in-Law, it's good to be back. You must not bother about tea."

"Yes—have a cup of tea."

Fay poured a cup of tea and Fook picked it up himself and sipped it. By this gesture Fook told Fay that since they were of the same generation, formalities need not be accorded him. Such was their relationship; courteous, yet free within limits of taste in their conversation, knowing the rules of behavior between brother and sister-in-law, yet understanding when to follow and when to relax the rules. On the other hand, from the first day in San Francisco, Fay had offered tea to Grandfather Kwong in the traditional manner with both hands holding the cup, and Grandfather Kwong, until his last day in San Francisco, had reciprocated with both hands accepting the cup.

Suddenly a sweet, childish voice sounded: "Second Uncle, Second Uncle, come in to see me!"

Fook set his cup of tea down and headed for the children's bedroom. Lin was sitting up in bed, dressed in a pink flannel nightgown, her arms extended in welcome. Kiang was deep in sleep. Fook went to Lin, his face beaming, and they embraced, laughing loudly together. "Are all your little measle marks gone?" he asked. "Yes!" she answered.

From that day on he was her beloved Second Uncle, to be cherished above her mother and father whose love, unlike Fook's, was too often tempered with discipline. For Lin knew only that Fook was always cheerful and that he knew delightful rhymes in English, which she did not then speak, reciting in a loud voice with a heavy accent: "Ling alound the losies, pocketful of posies," or better yet to her ears: "Low, low, low your boat; gently down the st-leam!"

She knew only that he was rotund of body, moon-round of face, that his voice was always loud, and that he loved rich food and drank much herb brandy. But in years to come she was to learn that he loved the feel of lustrous jade and fine porcelains even more than he loved wine; that though his voice was always loud, he could quote softly the words of Confucius and Mencius; in years to come she was to learn that those small hands were the hands of a connoisseur which, passed once lightly over a porcelain vase, would know its complete history.

In the person of her short, round uncle, Lin was to learn, was the soul of an artist, or in his words loud and clear that she heard him cry out one night in a tipsy mood: "I look like a second-rate cook in a third-rate chop suey house but remember the words of the sages of old: 'Beautiful women suffer an evil fate; intelligent men are seldom handsome!'"

LIN SAT UPON A HIGH WOODEN STOOL, A WHITE TOWEL tucked around her neck, moving not an inch while Fay trimmed the fringe of hair across her forehead. Early next morning, Fay, Kiang and Lin were sailing to China to the House that Tai Ming Built. Suddenly the black kitten leaped from the floor and scratched viciously at Lin's leg. She jumped up in pain and the sharp points of the scissors gashed her forehead. In the excitement Fay slipped and fell to the floor, twisting her ankle. Kiang, hearing their cries, rushed into the room and banged his head against the kitchen door. Thus once again the trip to the House that Tai Ming Built was postponed.

The doctor had come and gone. The children were fast asleep; Sun and Fook were below in the store. Fay lay in bed, deep in thought. She was a fatalist, and believed all things and events were determined by fate and that heaven had its reason for what it decreed. Now she wondered why, time and time again, fate had intervened to prevent her own and the children's trip to China.

One year it had been chicken pox, another year mumps, then scarlet fever, and then that terrible year when they thought Lin was going to lose her hearing when complications set in with the measles. In between these childhood diseases there had been a broken arm and a broken leg. One year Kiang had been hit by an automobile; the following year Sun had caught pneumonia. And there had been her three miscarriages, following closely one after the other, leaving her weak and unable to have any more children. And today, with their trunks already out of the house, there had occurred the almost comical accident caused by the new kitten Lin had brought home only yesterday. She sighed in resignation, for the trip would have to be postponed once again for another year. In her fall to the floor her weak uterus had been further disturbed and her doctor of Western medicine had prescribed treatment and long, undisturbed rest.

She closed her eyes and a smile spread over her smooth, unlined face. What does fate have in mind, she wondered? Next year, yes, next year fate would be kind; she was certain. Nothing more could happen. But the following year when all were healthy and in one piece, after their trunks had been sent out and their suitcases were ready, a cablegram would arrive at the Tai Ming Company saying that the dreaded disease of smallpox had broken out in their village. Once again their trip would be postponed. Nor would fate be kind the following year when word would come that Fay, Lin and Kiang must not return, for mad dogs were roaming about, that the whole frightened village dared not leave their homes, and that two children had died violently from attacks by the rabid animals. Then would come the worst blow of all—China's war with Japan

which ended all plans for Fay, Lin and Kiang to sail to
the House that Tai Ming Built.

Fay pushed herself up gingerly to a sitting position on
the bed and reached over to a table to pour herself a cup
of tea. She drank slowly, still deep in thought. During her
first several years in San Francisco she had longed to return
to her native land. Then the early intense yearning had
subsided and to return would have been not so much a
placating of a deep urgency as the pleasant experience of
once again living in the land of her childhood. Now, as
she drank her tea, she admitted secretly to herself that she
was almost glad she was not leaving her home in San
Francisco. It would have meant separation of her children
from their father; it would have meant separation of herself from Sun, now so dear and close to her even if she had
never told him so, and even though he had never expressed
his devotion except in being so thoroughly good and
thoughtful.

She recalled that at one time she had longed to return
to China for the sake of Grandmother Kwong, who was
still patiently waiting to meet the children for the first
time, waiting to correct them, to select their teachers for
them, to enjoy them in her old age. Yet contrary to tradition, her not being able to oblige Grandmother Kwong
had not greatly disturbed Fay. She was not an example of
the classical filial daughter-in-law who must do all to please
her parents-in-law: to have many, many sons for them, to
serve and honor them, to be entirely subservient to them.
For Fay, with her sleek hair like rich brocade and her
small bones like shafts of fine ivory, was a mixture of the
old and the new. She was a product of modern China. Her
father had allowed her to have an education, although in

her marriage at the age of nineteen she had not met Sun until the day of the wedding. She was a product of modern China, where a generation before her, her mother's generation, girls' feet had been crushed in compliance with the tradition of dainty three-inch feet, and education had not been permitted in the belief that it is virtuous for a woman to be untalented.

Sun came into the bedroom, his serious face complicated with deep concern. He paused at the doorway, looking at Fay, yet saying nothing. She called his name and he walked over to the bed.

"Are you comfortable?" he asked.

"Everything is fine," she replied.

He lifted the lid of the teapot. "Your tea is almost all gone now. I shall make more and put the pot into a quilted basket so it will remain hot."

"I've had enough tea. It won't be necessary to make more."

"Perhaps later; later you may wish for more tea."

"Perhaps . . ."

"The doctor said you must remain in bed and rest for a long time," he said.

"Yes—such misfortune!"

"Ah! But these things are fated, what can we do!"

"Yes, all things are fated," Fay agreed.

Never did a day go by that similar charges to fate were made, for fatalism was their belief, Tai Ming's belief, the belief of all whose names were recorded upon the genealogical tablets in the House that Tai Ming Built. It was a belief as old as the earth of China, the belief of virtually all who walked upon the earth of China.

"Sun, please fix my pillow for me."

As he plumped up the pillow, he asked, "Is there any pain in the ankle?"

"No, there is no pain if I don't move it. How are the children? Have you fixed their blankets?"

"They are both fast asleep, well tucked in."

"Good!" She pursed her lips and her face was very serious. She said, "Sun, you must call on Mr. Fung tomorrow so the children can start their lessons beginning Monday."

"I will do that, but don't you agree that the children must rest awhile? The cut on Lin's forehead was quite bad and the bump on Kiang's head is the size of a duck's egg."

Fay could not help laughing briefly, but then she was serious again, saying with great emphasis, "But you will for certain see Mr. Fung tomorrow!"

Sun replied with equal emphasis, "Assuredly!"

And Fay said, emphatically again: "Tomorrow for certain! Then we can write home and the family's disappointment will be lessened with the knowledge that the children's education has been attended to."

Sun, with his arms folded together and his face like a stern schoolmaster, replied firmly, "Yes!"

Fay was no longer the quiet, soft-spoken, shy bride. She was now a woman who held her ground firmly in matters she thought important to her family, especially those which concerned her children. She had had no voice in the choice of the marriage partner chosen for her by her family. In her early days in San Francisco, the strange country, the new husband she was as yet unfamiliar with, and a natural desire to show respect to Grandfather Kwong by behaving with decorum had combined to make her withdrawn and retiring. Now her voice was beginning to be heard more and more as each of these elements disappeared and as the responsibilities of her home and children increased. But always it was a voice with the tone of a jade bell, not brass. And she never ruled so much with an iron hand as she did with a porcelain hand, a hand that never struck too hard, for she knew that if it did it would not only damage itself but also the object it struck.

Sun asked, "Would you like something to eat?"

"No, I'm not hungry."

"Perhaps some hot tea now."

"Yes, that would be good."

He took the porcelain teapot and started for the door and then stopped and turned to face Fay. The soft light from the lamp on the nightstand flared upward, illuminating her face. She was a study in black and white, and with her hair unknotted it fell to her shoulders, touching her coarse white cotton jacket that buttoned at the neck. He thought she looked just as she had on the day of their wedding. Her face was unlined and smooth, her features well formed and regular. Privately, he was happy that the trip had once again been put off. Realizing he had stood by the doorway too long, he turned away. The thought remained that he was glad she was still in San Francisco. Once more he turned to face her but only to say kindly, "It will be about ten minutes before the tea will be ready."

"Yes, not too much tea leaf," she said.

In a few minutes Sun returned, the pot of tea in a quilted wicker basket in one hand, a stack of magazines in the other. He set the pot on the table and began to leaf through the magazines showing pictures of Chinese movie actors and actresses.

"Fook just came home with these for you to pass the time in bed," he said. "He bought some toys for the children too."

"Ah, Second Uncle is indeed good of heart."

It would have been a violation of good taste for Fook to visit Fay in her bedroom; thus the small gift served as a get-well wish.

"Shall I pour your tea?" Sun asked.

"No, let it steep a little longer. You had better go back to the store."

"Yes," he agreed, for it was a nightly routine for him to work on his account books after dinner.

He bent down to adjust her pillow again. For a brief second his fingers touched her shoulder. She closed her eyes: she was happy she was still here in San Francisco. She rather suspected he was also glad; she wished she could hear him say so, then inadvertently she moved, causing a jab of pain in the ankle. She subdued a cry. He asked, with concern, "What is it?" She closed her eyes, waiting until the pain went away. She opened her eyes and said to him, "It was nothing," and already she had forgotten what it was she wished she could hear from him.

ONE ENTERS THE KWONG HOME BY WALKING UP A NAR-
row flight of stairs; the home is next door to and above
the Tai Ming Company. The smell of sandalwood joss
sticks is subtle at the bottom of the stairway, and the fragrance is like a graceful hand extended in welcome, beck-
oning one to hurry. At the top of the stairs one is greeted
by solemn-faced men and women in the large living room,
sitting in poses as stiff as the teakwood that frames their
likenesses. Sandalwood joss sticks burn for them; pyramids
of sweet oranges and tangerines in porcelain bowls are
offered them so they will not go hungry; cups of tea are
offered them so they will not be thirsty; a vase of pink
roses is offered them so that they will have beauty before
their eyes. The living room is modestly furnished: rattan
tub chairs here and there; a long rosewood table against
one wall underneath the ancestral portraits; a hand-carved
camphorwood chest under a window; a mah-jongg table
and four chairs in one corner; a porcelain vase here and
a neat pile of deep blue, soft-bound books there; and on

[94]

a small rosewood table, an ivory God of Longevity holding the Peach of Immortality. Looking out from the large living-room window one sees stately, red-bricked Old St. Mary's Church; over yonder, gentle slopes of green grass in St. Mary's Square; up and down the steep hill of California Street the little brown cable cars.

At dusk, the gilded dragon that entwines the tall street lamp on the corner suddenly looks alive as the light magically comes on. The string of swaying paper lanterns now dances suddenly in childlike glee as the inner glow of the lanterns burns bright. The organ music of evening service vibrates softly from the church; the clang clang of the cable cars rings in rhythm with the faraway clanging of golden cymbals somewhere in the distance; and like the tempo of southern Chinese music is the talk and laughter of Sons of Tong, for the southern Chinese loves to talk and loves to laugh and when he talks his voice is loud and clear, his laughter spirited and hearty.

Towering above the natives of the Chinese quarter are the tourists: Middle Westerners looking for dark opium dens and pretty, helpless slave girls, nonexistent now though once they abounded on old Dupont Street; a couple from South Dakota staring at the characters on a piece of pink paper taped to a store window—they wonder what it reads. It reads: "Newly arrived; fresh turtles for soup, on sale here." Tourists from the New England states, from the deep South, admiring a hand-carved, camphorwood chest from Canton, settling instead for a ten-cent, wooden back scratcher. Tourists getting in the way of the busy Chinese housewives in the food stores, gaping and holding their noses at the sight of live snails in large buckets of water, salt fish in pools of thick oil, a ring of dried oysters hanging from a large nail on the wall, dried squids dangling in a bunch in the air. What in heaven's name is that? a lady from Wisconsin wonders; oh, lady from Wisconsin, something to put your canned soup to shame: the small intestines of pigs to make wonderful, wonderful soup! Tourists in a restaurant, eating fried noodles, fried prawns, and fried rice with silver forks; do they see how totally different their meals are from that of the Son of Tong next to them?

And high up in a large living room where lingers a fragrance of sandalwood and where the clanging of the cable car outside sounds like a toy bell, a family of five sit in rattan tub chairs drinking chrysanthemum tea sweetened with sugar. It is the hour after the evening rice, and Fook—Kwong Li Fook—is telling true stories of famous and infamous beauties of Old China.

". . . the brave Hua Mu-lan, who disguised herself as a man, and fought side by side with soldiers for twelve years; the Empress Wei of the Tong Dynasty who poisoned her own husband to gain the Dragon Throne; the beautiful Fei Yen of the Han Dynasty, whose lover hid under the bed when the emperor suddenly entered the chambers —that lover who unfortunately sneezed at the wrong time and was dragged out and his head abruptly severed from his poor body right there and then. And what of that superb beauty of all ages—Yang Kuei Fei? Yang Kuei Fei—" with awe Fook repeated the name of the fabulous beauty of the Tong Dynasty.

The serious-faced Sun interrupted, his voice low—the voice of a moralist: "Yang Kuei Fei, Yang Kuei Fei. Destroyer of a mighty emperor. A vain and lustful woman. The people starved so she could dine from platters of gold and drink from cups of jade."

But Fook blissfully ignored the words of the moralist and continued loudly: "Yang Kuei Fei, who looked into a bronze mirror set in rhinoceros horn to see cheeks of hoarfrost, lips of cinnabar, eyebrows of butterfly wings, and blue-black hair that flowed to her slender waist. She had a voice of music, a body like a willow. She dressed in floating robes of finest silk and walked in shoes encrusted with precious stones. And the mighty Emperor Ming Huang was madly in love with her and played on a flute of jade to her in the pavilions of the Imperial Palace."

And Sun interrupted again in his low, low voice, "And the mighty Emperor Ming Huang neglected his duty to his people and the affairs of his country for this evil woman and steadily emptied the treasury so that she could ride about haughtily in jade chariots and pink and white marble boats."

But Fook rose from his rattan chair to take over the story, his small hands moving with grace as he talked: "The beautiful Yang Kuei Fei made the emperor very happy. She danced for him, composed poems and melodies for him and sang sweetly to him. She loved him so much that to expiate for an occasion of offense to the emperor, she cut off her blue-black hair and set it on a platter of gold to have it presented to the Son of Heaven. How he loved her! Though he had many, many other concubines in the palace, he loved only her. Yang Kuei Fei—she made the Emperor Ming Huang exceedingly happy."

Sun, his chin tilted slightly upward, spoke in low tones again: "Yes, she made him happy as she made many other people happy—all her kinsmen who were given high positions within the palace—her arrogant, scheming, power-hungry kinsmen. Yes, she made many people happy—all her many lovers. She made the barbarian An Lu Shan, her lover, very happy, the barbarian who in time captured the Imperial Throne and proclaimed a new dynasty."

Fook again: "The Emperor Ming Huang delighted her every day with rich gifts of gold and jade; a hair ornament in gold filigree, scent and rouge jars carved in jade. Brocade and silks were continuously woven for her; artists and artisans daily carved for her."

The moralist retorted: "For the love of this devil-woman the emperor did not know his people were taxed unbearably by his scheming ministers. For the love of this devil-woman the emperor did not see beyond the feigned stupidity of the scheming barbarian An Lu Shan until the rebellion broke out and the court had to flee the capital."

Motioning Sun to stop, Fook continued: "And bravely Yang Kuei Fei took flight with the emperor. The beautiful Yang Kuei Fei no longer dined on platters of gold, or drank from cups of jade, but bravely bore misfortune side by side with the emperor, eating gruel and sleeping in thatched-roof cottages upon beds of straw."

Sun again: "The emperor and his family took flight and the people grumbled that they were left with no defense, for the emperor had neglected all in his blindness. And wherever the emperor went his men pillaged food from the people. The people cursed and in time even the soldiers revolted and asserted that Yang Kuei Fei was responsible for all their miseries and that this devil-woman must die!"

And Fook: "Yes, the people cursed and shouted for her life and bravely Yang Kuei Fei said to the weeping emperor that for the sake of the Dynasty, yes, she must die!"

Sun continued, most sternly: "The soldiers had already

severed the heads of her kinsmen and shouted for her head. Arrogant, haughty and vain to the end, Yang Kuei Fei said, 'I will die but let not their soiled hands touch me!' "

Fook: "Vain—yes; but not arrogant, not haughty. How she must have trembled in fear and wept unceasingly those last hours of her life. Not arrogantly, not haughtily, but very bravely she took a white silk scarf from her beautiful neck, tossed it over the limb of a pear tree and hanged herself."

An untouched and impatient Sun, a finger pointing at Fook, retorted unkindly, "Yes, for she knew that if she did not do that the soldiers would have clawed her to death!"

Fook, his face turned toward the ceiling, said: "Her slim body swayed to and fro in the wind. Was there a scent of perfume in the air, I wonder—for she loved to be sweetly scented. And the Emperor Ming Huang stood there in front of the swaying body, his wide sleeve soaked with tears of pain."

Sun, his eyes toward the floor, his fingers drumming on the arm of his chair, said, "Yes, the Emperor Ming Huang stood there, an old man of seventy, there in front of the swaying body, weeping for the woman who had once been the concubine of his own eighteenth son!"

Fook rose from his chair to recite the end of this tale out of history with a sweep of his hands: "And the Emperor Ming Huang's spirit was broken forever, and he refused to reascend the throne his son had regained for him. He must have welcomed death then so he could join his beloved, and ah! he did die—of a broken heart!"

Amid the lingering fragrance of sandalwood and the faint clanging of the cable cars, the five members of the Kwong family were silent for a brief while. The story of

Yang Kuei Fei had often been told after the dinner hour. Now each one directed his gaze to the view outside, each savoring his reaction to the story.

Fay had been envious of Yang Kuei Fei's beauty but very doubtful of the blind, romantic love that was beyond her understanding; Fook had been indulging a fantasy, identifying himself with the emperor, enjoying an affair that he knew would never happen to him; Lin, with years of youth ahead, thought the story could be her own—with the exception of the hanging by a silk scarf on a pear tree; Sun, the moralist, was outraged by a woman he branded as totally immoral; and Kiang had been bored because earlier in the afternoon he had gone to a movie-house in the nearby Italian district where he had seen a roaring Laurel and Hardy comedy.

Applause sounded; it came from Lin. She stood up, her head held high, her voice jade-toned: "I applaud Father and Second Uncle. Allow me the honor of serving you both more tea." She held her short skirt as if it were a long gown of pure silk and walked with measured steps. She held the teapot gracefully, and carefully poured tea for Sun. Slowly she walked over to her uncle Fook. He extended his cup and as she poured tea she smiled into his face. It was a mere hint of a smile, her pretty mouth did not open, and at that moment they both knew she was the courtesan Yang Kuei Fei.

This was the hour after the evening rice when the family gathered in the living room. This was the hour when tea was taken in leisure, lively tales told, harmless gossip unfolded, and when stories told of the magnificent House that Tai Ming Built made it as real a place as their modest home in the Chinese quarter of San Francisco.

China was now at war with Japan. No more plans were

being made for Fay, Lin and Kiang to sail to the Hills of Tong. Fook made no more trips abroad. Immigration attorneys had been consulted so that his wife and children could come to San Francisco, but his wife was filial and refused to leave, writing to ask who would care for all the old people if she were to leave the Hills of Tong. So in the House that Tai Ming Built, all genealogical records and valuables had been buried beneath the ground and the family prepared to flee to the hills if the Japanese should invade their part of the country.

Lin and Kiang were no longer little children. Through the years, the House that Tai Ming Built had been faithfully informed as to their education. The last letter to Grandmother and Grandfather Kwong told that Lin and Kiang were both doing well in high school and that the American system of education presented no problems of teachers or enrollment.

In contrast, Lin and Kiang's Chinese education had met with difficulties. When very young they had had a succession of teachers at home. Then followed several years at the town's largest Chinese school, which they attended along with hundreds of other pupils after their day in American school was over. Then for a year or two they had gone to a teacher who lived above a store and whose two dozen pupils climbed a narrow stairway to a loft furnished with long dark tables and benches. The room was windowless but brightly lit by naked bulbs. Because his pupils were in various grades, the teacher followed a rigid schedule to enable him to conduct each class separately. Being the disciplinarian that he was, the pupils who were not for the moment directly under him were always quietly reading their assignments or composing their themes.

Now for the past year and a half a private teacher once more came to the Kwong home to teach Lin and Kiang. He was not by profession a teacher but his health had become a problem and he had agreed to accept Sun's offer to teach the children. After an hour or so of uninterrupted lessons, Mr. Chin liked to digress and talk briefly about Confucius and Mencius. Encouraged by Lin's eager interest, the kind and mild-mannered man enlarged on these brief talks so that each evening during the last fifteen minutes he would chant softly the words of wisdom of China's two oldest philosophers, pausing often to explain in the vernacular the classical passages to his young pupils.

Chinese lessons for Kiang and Lin at home started punctually when the town siren blew at four-thirty and ended punctually at six-thirty. About the round kitchen table, teacher and students sat, while at the other end of the room Fay prepared dinner as quietly as possible. If either Lin or Kiang chose to keep their eyes on the cook rather than the lesson, Mr. Chin would move a finger lightly, for he was a gentle man who spoke in a soft, asthmatic voice.

At six-thirty, Mr. Chin would get up abruptly, followed by Lin and Kiang. Fay would walk over and without fail she would say, as she had said since the first day Mr. Chin had come to the house, "Teacher, are you through with the lessons?"

Mr. Chin would say, as he had said since the first day, "Madame, we are through."

"Teacher, won't you stay for dinner?" she would ask again, as she had asked every night.

"Madame, you are kind to ask but I have an engagement elsewhere," he would decline, as he had declined since the first day.

"Another day, then."

"Another day," he would promise again, talking as always with his eyes averted from Fay's eyes.

Fay would instruct Kiang and Lin, as she had since the first day, "Lin, Kiang, thank your teacher."

"Thank you, Teacher."

Teacher would nod his gray head, a faint smile showing through his silver-rimmed glasses. Fay would then follow behind Mr. Chin to see him to the door, saying along with her children in farewell, "Tomorrow we will meet again."

Now a problem had come up. Mr. Chin had given notice that he would no longer be able to come to the house to teach. His health was improved and he had accepted a full-time position with the Chinese newspaper. It was a difficult problem, for private teachers were scarce, and scarcer still was one who taught beyond the high school level that Lin and Kiang had reached.

CRAB WAS IN SEASON AND IT WAS BEING SERVED AS A LATE treat. The problem of a teacher would be discussed at this time. Four large crabs had been cooked in two different ways: crab curry, the color of pirates' old gold, smothered under large wedges of onions, green peppers and tomatoes; steamed crab, primarily for the benefit of Fay's more delicate stomach, the crabmeat to be dipped in a red vinegar sauce where long slivers of crisp green onions floated to give it an added flavor. Claws and legs were in large porcelain bowls ornamented, coincidentally, with a pattern of crabs and shrimps. Extra white napkins and glasses of water were ready for the occasion. Earlier, in answer to Lin and Kiang's pleas, Sun and Fook had gallantly relinquished their favorite part of the crab to the two young people who now gazed happily at the top shells that stood like bowls upon the table. Lin and Kiang would take spoon in hand to eat the soft meat and creamy juice. Tonight each had two top shells to revel in.

"We can enroll them in the Chinese school," said Sun, as he picked up a nice crab leg for Fay.

"But they are beyond the level of the highest grade in any of the schools," said Fay, ignoring the present of the leg, for she really did not like crab very much.

"Mother, I don't believe we need any more Chinese lessons," volunteered Kiang, one hand holding on to a side of the top shell, the other hand dipping the spoon into the liquid.

"Indeed!" said Fay, still ignoring the leg.

"Mother, let me explain. I have had to study twice as hard to maintain my grades in American school with the time I had to spend on my night lessons. Soon I'll be entering the University of California and I must have more time to study," Kiang, an honor student, implored.

Fook, looking cross-eyed as he stared at a large claw at close range, was sympathetic: "Sister-in-Law, there is truth in what Kiang says. I have always been amazed that Kiang continues to bring home such an excellent report card from school, with the time he has had to spend on his Chinese lessons. I doubt if I could have done as well in my youth. Elder Brother, do you recall that in the Hills of Tong we had an opportunity to study English in school but we didn't, for we thought it would be too difficult."

The faintest of smiles was on Sun's face. "Yes, that and the fact that our elders preferred that we had a pure Chinese education."

Fook: "How I wish that in our days it had been compulsory to study English. Yet on the other hand, I recall that those who studied English, when they spoke it frequently had to inject words of Chinese to express themselves completely."

Sun: "I recall—I recall—ah! this crab curry is marvel-ous!"

Fook: "If Kiang feels that he needs the time to study, my sympathies are with him. There is almost nothing in Chinese that Lin or Kiang cannot read. The letters they write home satisfy their grandmother and grandfather. They are not ignorant about the history of the Middle Kingdom. They have done very well! Ah! indeed the crab curry is marvelous!"

"Perhaps you are right, Second Uncle. Sun, do you agree?" asked Fay, finally getting to the leg as she tore the shell with nervous fingers.

Sun's head nodded in agreement, for his mouth was full of green peppers and onions. "Perhaps it is just as well to discontinue the lessons. It will almost be impossible to find a teacher at the college level."

"However, we will enroll Lin in one of the schools," said Fay, not realizing she made a face as she chewed the crabmeat.

"Mother, as you said a while ago, our lessons have gone beyond the level of the highest grade in any of the schools. If I have more time for my American lessons my grades will improve," said Lin, who took her studies at a leisurely pace. She took a swallow of water, for the curry was strong.

"True—true."

"Ouch!" cried Fook. His teeth had sunk too quickly into the shell of a large leg with a chunk of the body attached; the body had poked his right eye. He held the offending leg at arm's length and queried loudly: "Still alive? Is it so or is it not so?"

The matter was settled. Neither Lin nor Kiang would need to continue with the Chinese lessons. The eating of crab continued noisily as shells were cracked and exclamations of excellence sounded. Finally all that remained were mounds of pink and white shells.

"Kiang, Lin, write a letter to your grandfather and grandmother to explain the decision about your Chinese lessons."

Lin and Kiang took out ink brushes and paper to write the news to Grandfather and Grandmother Kwong. Through the years Grandfather Kwong and Lin had kept up a lively correspondence. He still called her Mui Mui and always began his letters with the sentence, "On this day as I sit in the pavilion upon the hill, I take up brush and paper to write to a dear one across the Pacific." Of late he had added a new note: "It is fortunate that I am still here in this beautiful garden. Let us hope Fate remains kind and that we will not have to flee to the hills. . . ."

Kiang's letter was finished in less than half an hour.

"Already?" asked Fay.

Lin, brush in hand, looked up to say: "Doubtless Elder Brother has written it in the vernacular style. To show Grandfather and Grandmother that we deserve the decision taken, I am composing with care a lengthy letter in the classical style." She returned to her writing, first dipping the brush into the ink box. Fay, Sun and Fook, but not Kiang, smiled discreetly and nodded their heads in approval. Spotting a leg that had somehow escaped everyone's eyes, Kiang snatched it, cracked the shell and began eating noisily.

A VERY SPECIAL GUEST WAS IN THE KWONG HOME FOR
dinner. At the round table with the family was tall, blonde
Val Beeson sitting between Lin and Fay. Directly opposite
Val was Sun, most self-consciously correct with his hands
in his lap, now and then attempting a faint smile directed
at the guest. Next to Sun was his round-faced brother
Fook, smiling broadly, opening a pottery jug of wine held
against his chest. Kiang, or Ken as he was called by his
fellow students at the University of California, was bent
over in his chair, leaning close to the table to tell Val that
his uncle's herb brandy was the most powerful drink in
the world. Kiang, alert-looking with dark eyes and brows,
long of face and slim of body much like his father, was now
a senior in the School of Business Administration. Lin, also
a student at the University of California, called her fellow
classman's attention to the porcelain rice bowls with the
pattern of the Eight Immortals. Val's light gray eyes, always hungry for color, grew wide with interest.

Fay, seemingly ageless, now turned to Val to say in Chinese, for she spoke no English, "Please partake of the

[108]

food," and her slim hand slowly waved over the food to pantomime to Val what her words could not convey.

Serving spoons had been produced for Val's benefit. An hour before, all of Fook's merry attempts to teach Val how to pick up food with ivory chopsticks had failed. The efforts of both teacher and student had been valiant.

"Wooden chopsticks, Val, we will try wooden chopsticks this time! They are not as slippery!"

And Val had tried as all watched eagerly. "I almost made it! I almost made it!" Val had cried when the piece of uncooked green, serving as a model, fell to the table when only an inch away from her mouth.

Still Val was to use porcelain bowl and ivory chopsticks at Fook's insistence that native food tasted best from native utensils. Fook's instructions were: "Val, scoop the food with the spoon and put it in your bowl. Now put the bowl of rice close to your mouth. You must smell its good aroma, you must feel its heat. With a pair of ivory chopsticks, shove the rice and food into your mouth again and again until your mouth is full and then chew and taste the fluffy goodness of our rice and the crisp texture of our food."

Now porcelain bowls with steaming hot rice were in everyone's hands and chopsticks were extended to pick up meat or greens from the common dishes in the center of the table. The considerate eater would pick food only from the area closest to him, and eat it without putting the chopsticks in his mouth. He would dip his soup spoon only a little below the surface of the common tureen and sip the liquid from the edge of the side of the spoon. Were a Son of Tong present as a guest Fay would have picked up food with her chopsticks and placed it in her guest's bowl as the dinner went along and this would please the guest, for this was the utmost in courtesy and consideration in dining with those from the Hills of Tong.

Were a Son of Tong present as a guest he would occasionally extol the excellence of the dinner between a spoonful of soup and lively biting of the food. "The greens are just right!" he would say, for Sons of Tong do not like their greens soft. "The seasoning on this dish is perfect!" he would exclaim appreciatively, for no salt and pepper would have been placed on the table. The hostess would be happy she had done well for she would have cooked by instinct, without benefit of cookbook, measuring spoons, measuring cups, or timing devices. The guest would urge his hostess's children to have more and more soup, telling them it was good for their health. Often this was winter melon soup, or watercress soup, or white cabbage soup, all containing plenty of nourishment.

Fay saw a particularly plump piece of white-meat chicken, picked it up with her chopsticks and put it in Sun's bowl. Sun, knowing it was an extra good piece, picked it up with his chopsticks and put it in Fay's bowl, telling her to have it instead. Fay noted that Val was enjoying herself, seeming to prefer the pieces of boneless squab cooked with large pieces of pecans. Fay said: "Tell Val to have more of the squab." Fook, now the color of a red rose, extended his chopsticks to the dish of squabs. He paused, for he was reminded of the varying viewpoints on the matter of sanitation; then he inverted his chopsticks and picked up two pecans and a piece of squab in one operation and put them in Val's rice bowl.

"Thank you, thank you, Mr. Kwong," said Val, her large face flushed by all the attention. She turned to Fay to compliment her on her talents. The words were translated for Fay who turned to Sun to say: "She is indeed a well mannered girl." Sun nodded in agreement and in halting English said to Val, "You are very kind."

Dinner was over and all went out to the living room. Sun and Fay sat in rattan chairs to have their tea. By the window, a group formed, standing to look at two canvases on two separate easels. Earlier in the day Val had painted the strings of paper lanterns swaying outside in the winter wind, while Lin reproduced on canvas the House that Tai Ming Built, using a photograph to work from. This mutual interest in color and form had brought Lin and Val together when they met for the first time in an English literature class.

"Rather amateurish I think," said Kiang of Lin's work. She shrugged off his opinion good-naturedly, for to her he was not a person possessed of any aesthetic taste.

"The colors are good, I think," he said of Val's work.

"Never mind, Ken. Uncle, we want your opinion."

Fook took a small step forward. He was the shortest in the group for now Lin stood almost a half a head taller than he and Kiang had grown taller than his father, but Val towered above everyone else. Turning from canvas to Val, Fook said in heavily accented English: "Val, this is a most delightful painting! That beautiful sky reminds me of the Chinese description of the lovely blue sky after gentle rain when seen between the floating clouds. The suggestion that it is a windy day is especially good in the last three lanterns!"

Now to Lin he said: "You are improving! You are less timid now, I see. There is more life and spirit in your work. I will say no more. Continue to paint and paint and someday better eyes than mine will judge your work."

They went to join Sun and Fay, everyone now sitting in rattan tub chairs forming a circle. Jasmine tea was served and it warmed all on this cold December night, the week after the bombing of Pearl Harbor. Val was completely captivated by Fay and asked permission to make a sketch of her. Surprised and flattered, Fay obliged and cooperated by moving her chair opposite Val. Pad and charcoal stick in hand Val began to sketch.

Small-boned and slender still, her face as yet unlined, maturity showed in Fay's large steady eyes. As always her face was lightly dusted with a soft shade of powder, her lips touched with a blotting of red paper against her mouth rather than lipstick. Her black hair was smooth and flat at the top, pulled behind at the ears and knotted in a chignon in the back. Small jade earrings were worn in her pierced earlobes. A cup of tea was within easy reach. Although she loved tea she drank none now and her hands were in calm repose upon her high-collared dress the color of old vintage wine. Fay's hands would appear in the sketch for they were lovely hands, lovely porcelain hands that had ruled that Lin's opportunity for education must be equal to her brother Kiang's, over the mild objection of Sun who had first questioned, then accepted, saying in the end, as if he had never objected: "Indeed Lin shall go on to a college education. Knowledge for the sake of knowledge is worthy, and opportunity should be denied no one."

It was the argument Fay had used to persuade him, though Sun had paraphrased it in his own way; nevertheless, very kindly, Fay had said, "Sun, that is splendid reasoning!"

All looked on at artist and model, Sun in secret admiration of his wife, Fook doubting the ability of a student to catch the essence of his sister-in-law. While the sketching continued, the men turned to talk of the war. America had declared war against Japan. How would it affect China, who had so long been at war with the Land of the Rising Sun?

"It may mean China will know peace sooner. . . ."

"The British! Will the British be able to protect their colonies in the East? If not, it may mean more Japanese conquest which may then prove even more disastrous for the Middle Kingdom!"

Kiang said, "America and China together will crush the Japanese in less than a year's time!"

"Kiang, who can tell? Who can tell? How can we know their true military might? Surely they must have been years in preparation for this!"

Then Sun began to talk of Japan's old and persistent ambition to conquer all of China, speaking with strong emotion. Fook frequently interjected, in the condescending tone of one who knew well the culture and arts of Japan. Fook's two oldest sons were university students; his other children were in high school, all studying in the British colony of Hong Kong where most of the larger schools of Canton had moved. They had often written to Lin, at times in English, but their letters in Chinese told more and told better of life in war-torn China.

Fay listened, her expression changing for the artist, as she thought of her own people and her people by marriage in the Hills of Tong. With the exception of Grandfather Kwong, all were safe and well in the village. Since the year when Grandfather Kwong and the family had fled to the hills the elderly one had not been well. In his flight he had stumbled and fallen heavily and since then his arms and other parts of his body often caused him great pain.

The sketch of Fay was finished. All went to see it at a closer range. "I haven't done justice to her," Val apologized, but all were polite and said it was well done. Fook took a chair next to Val and began asking her about her ambitions. Lin watched them as they talked together, a hand on her tapered chin, at times moving her hand to smooth back the long hair she wore in deep waves. She kept her eyes on them, thinking they were fast becoming her two favorite people, the two people most closely connected with a dark incident in her young life: When she and Val had applied for admission in a residence club for a weekend, Lin had been told, "This place excludes foreigners." Val's hands in comfort had been on hers and together they had left.

Telling about it to Fook later, he had called upon his reading to tell her: "When you have been treated in an unreasonable manner, ask yourself: did this happen because I lacked benevolence? Now turn to the offender and behave with benevolence; behave with propriety. Still you are treated in an unreasonable manner. Ask yourself again: did I try hard enough to be benevolent? Now turn to the offender again and do your utmost. Still you are ill-treated. Now turn your back to the offender and say to yourself: should I vex myself about such a wild beast?"

The wise words of Mencius, spoken centuries ago, remained with her and helped to wipe out the hurt, but a small scar of that painful incident always remained.

She now reached for the teapot and her cup and while pouring heard Fook say, as he jumped up from his chair: "Val, I will show you some of my books on Chinese art. Also, some pieces from my collection. Would you like that?"

"I'd love to see them."

Lin, after a sip of hot tea, turned to Val to tell her what splendor was in store for her.

THE SCENT OF BURNING JOSS STICKS MINGLED WITH THE aroma of white wine. It was the anniversary of a relative's death and earlier in the morning Fay had attended to the proper rituals with dedicated care and attention.

Over in a corner two rattan tub chairs were placed close to each other. On the side of one chair a small table was set with a dish of sweet tidbits, a pot of tea and two porcelain cups. All was in readiness for an important visitor on this bright but chilly December afternoon.

The doorbell sounded. Fay, looking slightly round of figure today because she wore a teal-blue silk dress lined with lamb's wool, with long snug sleeves, went to open the door for her expected guest.

Fay looked downward at her visitor, a short, old woman dressed all in black. "Grandmother, you have come."

The old woman, smiling broadly, a large package in her hand, replied in greeting: "Aunt, yes, I am here. Have you had your noon rice?"

The visitor was not related in any way to the Kwong

family, but because she was in her venerable eighties, Fay had accorded her the respectful title of "Grandmother." Flattered by this deference Grandmother had kindly chosen to address Fay as "Aunt."

Grandmother handed Fay the package. Fay peeped inside the bag and exclaimed: "Oranges! Grandmother, you are too good of heart. You should not have bothered!"

Waving her thin hands, Grandmother protested, "It is only a little thing I give you."

They walked into the living room, Fay directing the old woman with a hand. Grandmother had bound feet and as she walked, one foot pointed east and the other foot pointed west. Her arms were held stiffly by her side, the hands held upward as if braced by invisible supports.

Fay bade Grandmother sit down.

Grandmother asked, "Am I intruding in your daily routine?"

"No, you are not intruding."

"If you have dishes to wash, or food to prepare, don't allow me to occupy your time. You must go ahead."

"I have nothing to do and my time is free."

"Ah, you have done your noon's work!"

"Yes, I have done my noon's work."

Such a conversation was usual even between friends of a decade's standing, even if they had visited each other only yesterday, and the day before yesterday.

Fay said, "I will be but a minute in the kitchen while I slice these oranges."

Fay's small nose twitched slightly as she found that each of the six oranges in the bag was wrinkled and dry with dark spots on the peel. She shrugged her shoulders; Grandmother was a poor woman. Unfortunately, she had no oranges of her own to replace the bad ones. Gingerly she selected three that were slightly better than the others and proceeded to slice them and arrange them on a dish. The sliced oranges were dry and whitish-looking but nevertheless she carried the dish out with care and extolled the fruit.

"The oranges are very good."

She extended the dish to Grandmother.

Grandmother raised an old hand and said, "A little later, a little later. Put the dish on the table. We can get to them later."

Fay poured a cup of hot tea and offered it to Grandmother, who took the cup with both hands, nodding her head as she accepted it.

"Have some sweets," invited Fay, the plate of tidbits in her hands.

The steam from the hot tea spiraled up before Grandmother's face as she scanned the sweets offered her. She selected coconut strips.

"Slowly, slowly, Grandmother, eat slowly; there is time enough. Help yourself to more."

Fay relaxed in her chair, waiting for Grandmother to finish before discussing the specific matter about which the old woman had come.

Grandmother had been a widow for twenty-five years and dutifully continued to wear a black band over her smooth hair, loose black blouse and trousers and black cotton stockings. She had a small thin face and the taut yellow skin across her prominent cheekbones was flecked with the brown spots of the very old. Her eyes held a perpetually startled look; her thin pursed mouth, when it broke out in laughter, revealed spectacularly white teeth, all of them false. Her voice was shrill but her speech genteel.

Grandmother concentrated on the sweets and helped herself to more. She then noticed that Fay was not sharing the refreshment.

In her shrill voice she asked, "Aunt, why aren't you eating?"

"I finished my noon rice just before you came. In fact, I believe I overate and it will be wise if I refrain from both tea and sweets for now."

"Aunt, in that case some oranges will aid you. Oranges are excellent for indigestion!"

"Grandmother, do not bother about me! My discomfort will go away soon enough!"

The solicitous Grandmother reached for the dish of orange slices and offered it to Fay. "Eat some! It will do your stomach good! It is my remedy whenever I suffer from overindulgence!"

The oranges were under Fay's nose. A frown of displeasure crossed her face, but was quickly checked as she cautiously reached for one. She began to eat, forcing herself to swallow it.

"Is it not sweet?" asked Grandmother.

"Very sweet. You are good of heart to spend money on oranges for me."

"Nonsense! A few mere oranges. Aunt, more oranges! At least two more slices, the equivalent of half an orange and your relief will be immediate!"

A brown-spotted hand holding the dish was once again under Fay's nose. One more slice of bad orange would surely be enough face-giving to the venerable lady. Fay ate quickly and announced brightly: "Ah, already my indigestion is gone! The sweet orange did indeed do just what you said it would. How very wise you are!" And in great relief she saw Grandmother beam brightly, set the dish down, and resume her sucking of the sweets.

Fay had met Grandmother a week ago at a wedding banquet. The bride had impressed Fay deeply; the young girl was not only pretty, but sweet and modest. Learning through gossip at the table that the bride and groom had been introduced to each other through the services of Grandmother, Fay had invited the old woman to call upon the Kwong home whenever it would be convenient. Besides acting as a "go-between," or marriage broker, Grandmother was also available for housework for those new mothers who still observed the rule that after birth a woman must remain in bed all day for a period of one whole month.

The plate of sweets was empty. Grandmother sat back in her chair, looking like one who had just finished a good meal after having been denied food for many a moon.

Grandmother yawned and put a hand to her mouth, not to conceal her opened mouth but to help the act along, for those from the Hills of Tong do not consider it necessary to apologize for acts prompted by nature or necessity. Next, she belched.

Suddenly a black-clad arm darted out and a thin, brown-spotted finger pointed straight at an ivory figure. "Aunt, is that a Buddha?" she asked shrilly.

Fay instantly saw Grandmother was mistaken. "No, it is the God of Longevity, holding his Peach of Immortality." Then a teal-blue clad arm darted out and a spotless finger pointed. "Grandmother, that is a Buddha!"

Grandmother saw instantly the piece she had mistaken the other to be. "Ah, yes! What beautiful things you have," she said.

Fay, who loved those pieces, replied modestly, "They are not really first-rate."

Now Grandmother said, "Aunt, you were so kind to invite me to your home."

"Grandmother, my son is currently studying at the University of California and will graduate next year in June. I am thinking that it is the right time to select a wife for him."

"Ah, you wish to take a daughter-in-law."

Fay nodded her head.

"Has he no one to whom he is paying attention at the moment?"

"There is no one."

"Nowadays the younger generation, and especially the native-born of this country, prefer a mate of their own choice; most American-educated ones insist upon that. Is your son so different?"

"Tradition will be observed in our family. It is a mother's duty to select a wife for her son and I am acting accordingly."

"Your son will not object?"

"If a suitable one is selected what objections can there be?"

"How true! I have someone in mind. A lovely girl! Eighteen years of age, tall enough for a girl, and proportioned well; honest of face, straight of features, graceful in her walk and talk. She was born in San Francisco but went to the Hills of Tong as a little child and came back here when the war with Japan broke out. A pretty girl, a filial girl; a bit shy but is that not a virtuous quality for a girl?"

"Indeed!" agreed Fay.

"Her father is a food merchant; a prosperous, good,

honest man. I have been acquainted with her mother for many years."

"When could the introduction be made?"

"The introduction! Ah, Aunt, it is not as in our days when we saw our man for the first time at the ceremonies!"

"The fashion is indeed changing."

"Indeed it is! I will talk to the parents tonight. I will come over tomorrow to tell you further news."

"Good!"

Kiang entered the room and Fay greeted him, "Kiang, you are home."

Kiang answered, "Mother, I've returned." Seeing Grandmother, a stranger to him, he acknowledged her presence by greeting her impersonally as "Madame."

Fay called out: "Kiang, you must call her 'Grandmother.' Grandmother is in her eighties." Now those from the Hills of Tong deem it an act of reverence to announce another's old age and the old person feels flattered by the honor. Indeed, Grandmother's age was the second thing she had announced to Fay after her introduction.

Kiang, his handsome dark brows raised in surprise, cried out in honest amazement: "Eighties? One could not tell you are in your eighties!"

Yet to hear that one does not appear as old as one's actual age was equally welcome and pleasing, so that Grandmother's eyes were small for a minute and her teeth showed in magnificent splendor as she laughed and denied she looked any younger than all her eighty-four years. She said, "Aunt, you are the young-looking one! Who could guess you are the mother of such a grown boy!"

Fay denied she was youthful-looking.

"Aunt, is this the son?"

"Yes, this is my son Kiang."

"Aunt, you have a handsome child!"

Fay denied he was a handsome child.

"Young One! You are a fortunate young man to have a mother who cares so much for you. Young One! Do you agree or do you not agree?" She did not bother for an answer from Kiang. She rose from her chair, slapping the back of her trousers as she straightened up. "Aunt, I must leave now."

"Can you not stay longer?"

"You are good of heart but I must leave. We will meet again tomorrow."

"Yes, we will meet again tomorrow."

Grandmother departed.

Kiang, hungry after the train ride from Berkeley, reached for a slice of orange. Fay called out, "Kiang, don't eat those oranges!" She took the dish into the kitchen and tossed the contents into the garbage pail.

It was the following day and once again Grandmother was at the Kwong home.

"Madame Chin, wishes you and your son to visit them tonight at eight o'clock. Madame Chin confided that she will not tell her daughter of the purpose of our visit. That will be to your advantage for she will be more her natural self if she does not know we are there to appraise her."

Fay was elated, then her expression changed. She slapped her hands lightly in disappointment. "Grandmother, this is the day Kiang has late afternoon classes so that he has dinner in Berkeley and then returns to the University library to study. It will be almost ten o'clock by the time he arrives home."

Grandmother's startled eyes became narrow and her head shook with frustration that her plans had failed.

Fay asked hopefully, "Will tomorrow be agreeable?"

In a cross voice, Grandmother said: "That is the problem! Madame Chin said it must be tonight. Her out-of-town relatives are arriving at her home tomorrow. From that day on she will not have a moment free. She must take her relatives to dinner, to the theater, shopping, to other relatives. Her guests will be at her home for one week. It will not be proper at all for us to appear at the Chin residence during that time."

Her woman's curiosity aroused, Fay felt it would be impossible for her to wait a whole week. She said, "The two of us will visit Mrs. Chin tonight. We will leave at seven-thirty."

Grandmother was pleased again. Her plans were going as scheduled, although the prospective bridegroom would not be coming in person. To Grandmother this was not important, after all; in the matter of selecting a wife, was it not for a mother to decide?

Fay returned home from the visit to the Chin family looking jubilant and pink-cheeked, for the chilly December wind had been sharp and strong. At once she sought out Sun and Fook and told them about the girl.

Her smooth lacquered hair was brilliant, her firm chin held high above the collar of her teal-blue silk dress as she talked in jade tones. "She is a most attractive girl but what impressed me more were her good, quiet manners. Not a bit of boldness in her! She knew instantly how to address Grandmother and me without having to be prompted by her mother. She knew how to serve tea, and the sweet dumplings offered us were of her own cooking and I must confess hers were even better than mine!"

Sun, his face stern but his heart warmed by the charming ways of his wife, said, "She sounds as if she will make a most filial daughter-in-law."

Stroking the tiny jade tiger that hung on a red silk cord looped to his belt, Fook interposed cheerfully, "She sounds like a very proper person." His opinion in this matter would be heard only when it was asked for because first of all, the selection of a wife was a woman's province; secondly, his own son was not involved.

Kiang arrived home laden with his leather zipper case and his books. "Father, Mother, Second Uncle," he called.

Fay said, "Kiang, there is a matter we wish to discuss with you." The story was unfolded.

Kiang listened respectfully, at first thinking Fay was not serious, toward the end realizing that his mother was indeed in earnest. He chose his words carefully. "Mother, you are good of heart to think of my future but when the time comes to take a wife, it must be one of my own choice."

Lin came out of her bedroom. All of the previous conversation was repeated for her benefit.

Fay said, "Kiang, I concede that the fashion in marriage is changing but there is no young lady you are serious about. It is not good for a grown son to remain single for long. So I am doing what is proper for a mother to do."

Kiang, stroking his Phi Beta Kappa key as Fook stroked his jade piece, said, "Mother, I wish to remain single for some time yet."

Kiang, a straight-A student since his freshman year, foresaw the day when his entrance into the Tai Ming Company would transform a small two-man business into a national concern. He would take out papers of incorporation and issue capital stock for sale to the public, the family to retain a majority ownership. Buyers would travel to

Hong Kong, Canton, Shanghai, Macao, Singapore and Manila for quality products. Teams of salesmen, both white and Chinese, would travel throughout the forty-eight states and Canada and their progress would be carefully watched by Kiang as he moved the pins that represented them on the huge map that would hang on the wall in place of the deceased ancestors' portraits. Sun's and Fook's present policy of oral agreements with their several wholesale customers would be replaced by written agreements made in triplicate; credit would be allowed only upon satisfactory Dun & Bradstreet reports; the system of the abacus and soft-bound account books would be thrown out and replaced with sleek IBM machines operated by efficient young women, both Chinese and white.

Also included in Kiang's plans for the Tai Ming Co., Inc., was the renovation of the family's present living quarters into executive offices, his own office to be the room where the family gathered nightly for tea. Often he had pondered: should his imported, custom-made blackwood desk face the view of the church and the park, or should customers and buyers have the advantage of the view? Kiang would still be the industrious Son of Tong, but westernized, squeezing his work into an eight-to-five, five-and-a-half-day week at a frenzied pitch; he would not be the industrious Son of Tong that old Tai Ming, Grandfather Kwong and Sun and Fook had been, whose pace was unhurried, whose spirit was noncompetitive, whose busy schedule was twelve hours a day, seven days a week, with hardly a thought of complaint that their only holidays in the year were the first two days of the Chinese New Year.

"Kiang, there will be no marriage until after your graduation. Would you at least come with me to meet the girl?"

"Mother, I would rather not."

Fay's porcelain hands clapped together and the pair of jade bracelets on her slender wrist produced a musical note. She was too astonished by her son's impudence to speak. Sun's finger waved sternly in the air as he said, "You may not speak so to your mother!" and his eyes were on Fay to see if her anger was thus allayed.

In properly remorseful tones Kiang said: "All right, Mother, I'll go and visit the family with you."

Fay was happy again. Sun looked at her and his face was soft and kindly. Why should his son object to a wife being selected for him? Had not all the men in their family had wives selected for them in the way millions and millions of other Sons of Tong had? Was he himself not exceedingly fortunate that the bride chosen for him and now the mother of his two grown children became more mellow in her beauty with the years so that now she seemed to him even more lovely and gracious than on the day of their wedding?

CLASSES WERE OVER FOR THE CHRISTMAS SEASON, NOT TO be resumed until the New Year. From the living room the family could see a life-size setting of the Nativity in front of the church. Across the park, red and green lights trimmed a sprawling tree. The family talked less during the hour after the evening rice as they listened to the organ music of Christmas hymns from the church.

A schedule whereby Kiang's free time was to be utilized in acquainting himself with the Chin girl had been imposed by Fay. Kiang had gone with Fay to meet the family. When home, it had been difficult for him to give an opinon of the girl when Lin pressed him for his reactions.

Kiang had replied: "I can't tell you more. She met us at the door and thereafter vanished out of sight for the rest of the evening. I sat while the older people made polite conversation. Once in a while she peeked in at us. She's a rather pretty girl."

It was arranged for Kiang to take her out for dinner and to the theater. The girl suffered from acute shyness and throughout the evening spoke not a word, only emitting a giggle whenever Kiang prompted her to conversation. Thereafter Kiang gave no further thought to her and concentrated on his studies, in preparation for the final examinations that would take place next year.

Fay took her son's silence for assent and, without letting him know, consulted with the Chin family about the marriage. Fay thought Kiang's noninterference was commendable; he was behaving as a proper son of the Hills of Tong, leaving these matters entirely in the hands of the women.

At the end of the semester, Kiang's mind was free to think of other things than International Money, Banking, and Case Analysis of Management Problems. To his astonishment he learned that his engagement to the Chin girl was soon to be announced. Already Fay was debating which baker was to get the order for the engagement cakes, and in which restaurant she would make reservations for a small dinner party.

Forgetting all that had ever been imbued in him, Kiang banged an angry fist upon the table and cried, "I will not have that child for a wife!"

Sun and Fay were speechless. Fook, stroking his jade tiger, shook his head in sympathy for everyone. The round-faced Fook believed in these marriages, yet he could understand in this day and age, and especially for one as westernized as Kiang, a man wishing to marry a girl of his own choice.

Remorseful, now that he realized in what a tremendously difficult situation he had placed his mother, Kiang said: "I cannot go through with this. I will not go through with this." Nervously he rubbed his Phi Beta Kappa key; if his grades continued on the same level, he would graduate with high honors in June.

Having neither a jade piece to stroke nor an honorary society key to rub, Lin, her hands gently massaging Fay's aching temple, asked her speechless mother, "What do we do now?"

The next day found a tired-looking Fay discussing the situation with Sun. Idea after idea was discarded. A solution was difficult; there was no precedent which they could call upon to follow.

Kiang came home late in the afternoon and announced: "I have volunteered for the United States Army. My papers are in order and I shall have to leave in another week's time."

Fay was heartbroken. Kiang stood before her, a dutiful son, and tried to lessen her unhappiness, "I would have been drafted into the army anyway, sooner or later."

Fay was finally able to speak. "We must not cause the Chin family any loss of face. We have almost brought them tremendous humiliation and this new development must be handled with the greatest delicacy. We must not tell them Kiang has volunteered for the army, but that he has been drafted. Am I right or am I not right?"

A long silence followed.

Sun stepped forward so that he was in the center of the group. His arms were folded together; his face was stern, his nose pointing slightly upward, like one about to discuss the decline and fall of the Chinese Empire. He began: "As I see it, this is the proper solution! We will inform the Chin family through Grandmother that Kiang has officially received word that he is to be inducted into the United States Army. Not one word must leak out that Kiang has volunteered. That would cause them a grave loss of face. We will say that any talk of marriage at this time must be postponed."

He looked at Fay for her reaction. Fay was very tired but even if she were not, her answer would have been the same; very kindly she said, "Sun, your idea is excellent!"

Sighs of relief greeted her words. Then Fay began again, "To make up for everything, we will invite the Chin family out for dinner as if to join us in sending Kiang off."

Five minutes elapsed as Kiang comforted his heart-broken mother. Then Sun called for attention: "Since we have had such intimate talks with the Chin family, it is only appropriate that we do not drop all matters so abruptly! Accordingly, I have decided to reserve two dinner tables and ask that they join us for Kiang's farewell dinner!"

"Excellent—excellent." Fay's voice, as kind as ever, was noticeably weaker.

It was the last dinner at home for Kiang. All his favorite dishes had been specially prepared for him. Tomorrow he would be a civilian no more. For the occasion, Kiang and Lin had been allowed herb brandy with dinner. When the meal was over, Sun and Fay left the living room to have their tea. Kiang, Lin and Fook remained at the dinner table drinking their wine. From the kitchen they heard the solicitous voice of Sun saying to his heartbroken wife, "All matters are fated. . . ."

The round-faced Fook refilled the wine cups. He said, his cup in midair: "Kiang, someday! Someday! Someday a girl of everyone's approval will be yours and the harmony between you two will be like a melody from the harp and the lute!"

The herb brandy was powerful so that now a drunken

Kiang suddenly cried out: "What have I done? What have I done? What a foolish thing I have rushed into! They might send me overseas and I might get killed!"

Lin looked at him with love. They were as different a pair as Sun and Fook and often at odds with each other—she forever saying that Kiang was too practical and he forever questioning the value of her education in the School of Liberal Arts—nevertheless, they loved each other.

She picked up her cup of herb brandy, put an arm around him, and after waiting for a hiccup to subside, said to him: "Elder Brother, don't worry even if you go overseas. You have Tai Ming's ears and the saying goes: If the space behind the ears does not permit a finger, the age of eighty will be passed. Second Uncle, Elder Brother, let us drink a cup!"

Part *Three*

❧ The Season of the Chrysanthemum

FOOK'S HANDS HAD LONG AGO STOPPED CLAPPING IN rhythm to the verses he sang in a loud, clear voice to Lin. To Lin, her uncle's small hands were never more graceful than when they held a fifteenth century piece of jade, his voice unhurried, and low as he spoke of its history, his moon-round face mellow and warm as he gazed lovingly at it.

It had all begun shortly after Lin's fifteenth birthday when the beauty of a blue-and-white vase in Fook's room suddenly struck her as exquisite. It had pleased Fook that she found the vase beautiful. It was a Ming piece, he explained, showing Lin the mark of the reigning Emperor Hsuan Te. Holding the thirteenth century piece, Lin ran a hand over and over the grain of the fine porcelain as Fook enlarged on why the design of pine, plum and bamboo trees appeared to swim under the glaze. Fascinating and romantic thoughts stirred in Lin's mind as she continued to hold the exquisite vase: what empress, what courtesan, what duke had held this vase hundreds of years ago; where in the Imperial Palace had it stood, and why, centuries later, did it stand upon an old table in a room in San Francisco?

Gently taking the vase out of her hands Fook said: "It is good that you admire this fine piece. I want you to know more of the true arts of China. Then you will know her greatness and her splendor; you will know of her people creating works of art centuries before the birth of Jesus Christ; you will know of a culture so superior that always her conquerors adopted it. To know the true arts of China is to know what a tremendous influence they have exerted on the arts of other countries in Asia and Europe."

Throughout the 1920's and the 1930's, when Fook made his annual trips to China to visit his wife and children in the House that Tai Ming Built, he accumulated priceless treasures of Chinese antiques. These he had stored in a large room, taking one or several pieces out at a time to enjoy.

In the city of Canton, merchants came to him with their antiques, both the genuine and the spurious, wrapped in bundles of blue cloth, and bargaining and arguing went on for hours when Fook's trained eyes spotted an unusual piece. Many of Fook's antiques also came from the sale of famous collections, broken up after the collector's death. In such sales collectors from all of China and Europe bid hotly against one another.

Fook also made many of his private purchases in Canton through Mr. Fong, who operated a lovely small shop on the Street of Heavenly Arts. Because Fook could always distinguish the genuine old pieces from copies, the first thing he requested was that Mr. Fong show him only the genuine pieces. Mr. Fong would chuckle at the knowledge that Fook realized his rascality but still continued to patronize him.

After a purchase of a Sung celadon, or an eighteenth century jade piece, Mr. Fong would invite Fook to a cup of jasmine tea. Then while they sat on blackwood chairs, drinking tea and chewing melon seeds, Mr. Fong would tell how just this morning he had sold an American matron a fake bronze vessel, supposedly a Shang piece.

Now the Shang-Yin Dynasty dates from 1558 B.C. to 1054 B.C. and bronzes of this period are highly prized by collectors, not only for their beauty but even more because they have remained in existence for so long. Ancient bronzes buried for thousands of years take on a patina that is greatly admired. The patina is of a blue-green, yellowish or reddish efflorescence. But new bronze can be given the same patina by soaking it in vinegar and oil, or a genuine patina can be taken from an ancient bronze and transferred with wax onto a new bronze. Also, many ancient bronzes have been sold as genuine pieces though they have been put together from the fragments of genuine bronzes found in excavations.

A very high price was asked of the American by Mr. Fong for the fake bronze. The matron, very excited and dripping cigarette ashes all over the beautiful red rug, obviously wanted the piece but was most reluctant to pay the price. Mr. Fong soon realized that she knew very little about Chinese art in that she raised no questions regarding the style, inscription or designs on the bronze, but merely repeated that the Shang-Yin Dynasty dated back to before Christ.

They haggled and bargained over the price until it seemed that she would give in. But just as she was about to pay, she asked once more to be assured she was buying a genuine Shang piece. Mr. Fong was about to open his mouth when the American threw a burned-out match onto the beautiful red rug. Then as Mr. Fong's heart raged, he beamed a broad smile and said that for everyone's peace of mind he would bring out the catalog. Mr. Fong took out a Chinese book, pretended to read and then made elaborate apologies. Said Mr. Fong: "Ah, it is not a Shang piece. I am deeply sorry. Humbly sorry." Said the matron, "What?" Said Mr. Fong, "It is an imitation of a Shang bronze done in the Sung Dynasty." Dropping more ashes on the rug, the American ranted and raved that she had almost been cheated out of a fortune until Mr. Fong explained that the Sung Dynasty dates as far back as the eighth century, A.D., and that these imitations were made not in any attempt to deceive but to have a copy of a much-admired piece of the past.

This satisfied the matron, who now repeated, "eighth century, eighth century." Bargaining was resumed, the matron refusing to pay the original price asked for inasmuch as it was only eighth century A.D. and thus much later than a Shang piece. Mr. Fong feigned helplessness and the deal was consummated with the American paying half of the original asking price, which of course was still high. Before she left she demanded assurance from Mr. Fong that the piece looked enough like a Shang piece to be passed as one. Mr. Fong pointed to the book and told her that it was stated there that even the best of experts would have difficulty telling the difference. Fook, knowing Mr. Fong for the knave he was, asked what he had used for the catalog. Mr. Fong burst out in ungentlemanly laughter and replied that it was his grandson's first grade reader.

In Grant Avenue, before America's entry into World War II, were stores called Nippon Trading Company, Nara Art Store, Yamamoto Curios. Japanese merchants outnumbered the Chinese merchants. Japanese merchants sold everything from cheap souveniers to the exquisite woodcuts displayed in Mr. Toguchi's studio next door to the Tai Ming Company. Fook often chatted with Mr. Toguchi, and the two merchants exchanged talks about their collections. Fook particularly admired the woodcuts which the ancient Chinese invented but which the Japanese had developed to a consummate art.

When the United States declared war on Japan and all Japanese were ordered evacuated from the West Coast, Fook negotiated for the purchase of Mr. Toguchi's studio, which was well known among collectors of oriental art. Mr. Toguchi, a United States citizen, was both indignant and deeply hurt by the evacuation orders, and like many other Japanese suffered great financial loss in his hurry to sell his home, business and personal property to meet the evacuation deadline.

In Mr. Toguchi's studio that was now Fook's were placed all the beautiful antiques that he had purchased in China. Like Mr. Fong's store in Canton that Fook admired so much, a beautiful red Chinese rug covered the floor. A pair of large blue porcelain Fo dogs guarded the door, as once they had guarded the home of a court official of the Ching Dynasty. Porcelain garden seats with designs of rocks and flowers stood here and there, and visitors were invited to rest on them while they looked at a painting or a Buddhist sculpture in stone.

The antiques were arranged in glass cases on black shelves against a simple background of off-white walls. Here was a Han pottery vase, its lines simple and flowing, cre-

ated by an artist born before Christ, the green enamel of
the vase oxidized by time and the earth to a fine silver
iridescence. Here were the bronzes of the Chou era: dagger
hilts, mirrors, chariot fittings, belt hooks. Here was an
ancient cicada-shaped jade amulet that once was used on
the mouth of a deceased person; Taoist figures in old ivory;
a black lacquer screen with an inlaid mother-of-pearl design of court ladies in a garden, a stone lion at the side of
the screen. On one wall was a monochrome painting of a
scholar in his mountain retreat; on the opposite wall, an
ancient silk scroll of fine calligraphy.

Here were Lin's favorite collections, the fine pieces
of pottery tomb figures of the Tong Dynasty made to be
buried with the dead for the deceased to use in the next
world: the Arabian horse, his long mane flowing and his
proud neck arched, from the tomb of a nobleman; the clay
replica of a dead man's wife, her belly swollen with child.
And Lin often wondered from whose tomb came the clay
replica of a dwarf once buried in it—was he loved by the
deceased, a dwarf whose head was grotesquely large and
whose legs were stunted?

And there were the porcelains.

Fook's favorite porcelains were the collections of the
Sung Dynasty, from A.D. 960–1279, simple, restrained,
serene and harmonious, although the Middle Kingdom
was then economically weak and insecure and constantly
threatened by barbarous tribes. The porcelains were simple in form, their colors delicate and monochromatic.

Here was a Northern celadon bowl, the glaze of an
olive-green shade with an incised pattern of leaves. Here
was a translucent Ting Chou bowl—undecorated, pure
white, smooth and velvety as white jade, made in white
for a household in mourning. Here was a Chien Yao tea

bowl, used by scholars in the Sung Dynasty for competitive tea-tasting games. Made to fit the hand, the glaze was a thick, lustrous black with streaks of silvery spots of oil. Here was a Chun Chow bowl upon a teak stand, simple and lovely, in a delicate shade of lavender.

In the collections of the Ming Dynasty, A.D. 1368–1644, the forms were bold, the colors glowing, reflecting a period of peace, material prosperity and expansion for the Middle Kingdom.

Here was a pure white, translucent porcelain dish made during the reign of Emperor Yung Lo that rang with a musical note when struck, with an incised design of a dragon catching a pearl visible only when the dish was held up to the light. Here was a blue-and-white vase with the design of the Three Friends, the pine, plum and bamboo trees. It bore the seal of the Emperor Hsuan Te, during whose reign this type of porcelain reached its greatest perfection for then "Mohammed Blue," a fine cobalt, was imported into China and mixed with the native blue.

Then there were the porcelains of the Ching Dynasty from 1644 to 1912, a time when the whole Empire of China was under the alien rule of the Manchus. This was when porcelains reached their zenith in beauty of design, brilliance of color, quality of material and perfection of technique. After an initial period of unrest, many brilliant Manchu emperors ascended the throne, notably Emperor Kang Hsi, Emperor Yung Cheng and Emperor Chien Lung, all great patrons of the arts.

During the reign of Emperor Kang Hsi were developed the beautiful monochrome glazes: *sang de bœuf,* peach-bloom, mirror-black, deep blue, powder blue, peacock green, eelskin yellow, pale gold, apple-green, iron-red, iron dust, and tea dust.

Also during the reign of Emperor Kang Hsi were created the enamel-decorated porcelains: the *famille verte* group—the enamels of jewel-like brilliance in green, eggplant, yellow, violet blue, and coral red; the *famille noire* and *famille jaune* groups—brilliant enamels against a background of black-green or greenish yellow.

During the reign of the Emperor Yung Cheng the *famille rose* was widely used, ranging from deep, deep crimson to pale pearl pink.

During the reign of the Emperor Chien Lung, new monochrome enamels and variations of existing colors were introduced: aubergine, yellowish green, opaque ruby pink, robin's-egg, turquoise, dark blue, crackled brown and buff, camellia leaf-green, emerald green, bronze green, tea dust and iron rust.

In Fook's studio, which he named the House of Tong, was a vase of the Chien Lung period decorated with *famille verte* enamels. The colors and lines were magnificent and Fook accorded this vase a place of honor, for it stood proudly alone in a pale green silk-lined case of teak.

LIN HAD COMPLETED HER THIRD YEAR OF COLLEGE AT THE University of California as a liberal arts student and was very happy to have the diversion of working for Fook at his studio that summer. Fay opened the brass lock of a camphorwood chest and with tender care brought forth lovely brocade jackets, some in the softest of pastel shades, some in the most vivid of colors; these Lin was to wear with a "little black dress." Down at the bottom of the chest that held such a wonderful fragrance were many fine pieces of silk, the colors and materials as fresh as on the day they were purchased in China. These were to be made into native dresses like those worn by Fay, with a high collar, frog buttons on the side, and slits on both sides of the skirt; this modern, short Chinese sheath was commonly known as a "cheongsam."

At Fook's suggestion, Lin's hair was brushed back smoothly at the top, pulled to the back, and the strand of long hair coiled to a chignon at the nape, just as Fay wore hers. When Fook saw Lin in a pale blue brocade jacket with wide sweeping sleeves, he nodded happily in approval. However, he said: "Lin, you should not wear a western black dress and black high heels; you are not completely authentic."

Lin shook her head and replied, "This is an expression of my soul, a bit of the East, a bit of the West; I have always found so much to love in both. . . ."

And while Fay clicked her tongue in disapproval, Fook praised Lin as she stood before him, putting on a pair of teardrop jade earrings: "Good, good, good! Indeed, our Lin is a beauty. But—but . . ."

"But what?" Lin asked.

"Something is indeed wrong. I shall be back."

In half an hour's time, Fook was back. In his small hands, he held two things: a slender bottle of the essence of lilacs and a copy of the Analects of Confucius.

He said: "The fragrance of lilacs, subtly sweet, youthful, most delightful; do you not remember how the famous beauty Yang Kuei Fei always loved to be sweetly scented. And coming up the stairs with this perfume I turned back for this book. A copy of the Analects of Confucious to remind you not to overlook the fragrance of one for the fragrance of the other. Remember your Grandfather; he said that from books can come fragrance as sweet as perfume."

With both hands extended, Lin gratefully accepted the book and the slender bottle of the sweet essence of lilacs.

Fook named his studio the House of Tong for one of the most brilliant dynasties in the history of China that lasted from the fifth to the ninth century A.D. Li Po, the poet lived during the Tong Dynasty. Many of the emperors of the period were artists themselves and encouraged literature and art. Emperor Ming Huang, who reigned in the sixth century, the same Emperor who loved the ill-fated Yang Kuei Fei, founded schools throughout the country and gave many people opportunities for education. It was a time when Arabs, Persians and Jews went to China to live and study. It was an era so great and glorious that the people of south China, including those in San Francisco who are virtually all from the province of Kwangtung, call themselves Sons of Tong.

Profit was not uppermost in Fook's mind. More than anything, he had established the House of Tong as a means to display some of the great art of China still unknown to many Westerners. All too many were the shops on Grant Avenue, now all operated by Chinese merchants, that carried the inferior items of ceramic dolls, back scratchers, and gaudy porcelain pieces. The shops selling these ugly things far outnumbered the few stores that handled good wares, wares such as were sold by the Tai Ming Company, objects of good taste made for commercial purposes; but here in the House of Tong, each piece had been fashioned when art was for art's sake and often created under imperial patronage.

The feel of beautiful porcelain, rich jade, old bronze, the stir felt from looking at a monochrome painting of a scholar's retreat in the mountains, Lin was to experience so that it seemed to her that nothing mattered in the world but lovely works of art. She read much that summer on the history of Chinese art so that she could know more about the pieces in the studio. With Fook's help, she read works dating back to the early dynasties including the classic series, The Mustard Seed Garden. She read books on Chinese art by Western writers. Bushell's famous *Chinese*

Art she constantly referred to. But Fook cautioned her about the possibilities of misinterpretation by these Western writers, and also their skepticism and unfair criticism of the Chinese who wrote on the ancient arts of China.

Lin was happy and busy that first summer, working from noon to evening. It was also in that summer that Kiang came home on furlough for a brief stay, confiding to Fook and Lin that he was to go overseas to the Pacific Theater when his leave was over.

For Lin, the hours went by quickly, day passing into night as smoothly as jade passed through her fingers. The four seasons of the year might have passed as pleasantly and unnoticed within the studio except that a young man was to come into her life. That summer she met Scott Hayes. She had thought that heart and mind were full; she was to discover how much more the heart could hold when love was hers in autumn, the Season of the Chrysanthemum.

THE FIRST VISITOR TO THE HOUSE OF TONG WAS MRS.
Evangeline Marshall. Gray-haired and lovely and always
fragrant with the perfume of lavender, she came in to inquire about the celadon bowl displayed in the small outer
window. She had stepped off the California Street cable
car and was on her way to Old St. Mary's Church. Then
she had noticed the Sung piece. Fook and Lin spent a
pleasant hour with her as she told about her Ming pieces
at home collected by her mother and father, who had
lived for a short time in Peking in the days of the old
Empire.

Mrs. Marshall, Fook and Lin became good friends. A
true San Franciscan, Mrs. Marshall loved to ride the cable
car down the steep hills, stopping on Grant Avenue to go
into Old St. Mary's Church and going from there to visit
the studio. No, she said to Lin and Fook, holding on to
a silver-tipped cane, she was not of the Roman Catholic
faith but she loved the quiet of the church.

One Saturday, an hour before noon, the telephone

rang simultaneously with the musical note produced by Lin's jade bracelet as it accidentally struck against a porcelain garden seat. She got up and laid down the feather duster to answer the phone. The voice on the other end of the line said she was Mrs. Hayes, Mrs. Evangeline Marshall's daughter; her mother's birthday was tomorrow and she was at a loss as to what to give her. What could the House of Tong suggest? She knew her mother had been a frequent visitor to the studio and was fond of Chinese things. Lin told Mrs. Hayes of a scholar's brush pot in blue-and-white porcelain which Mrs. Marshall had wanted to add to her collection.

"Wonderful! wonderful!" said Mrs. Hayes; it solved her problem. Could it be delivered immediately? Lin said they did not deliver. "Oh dear," wailed the voice from the other end of the line, "How can I give it to Mother in time for her birthday?" She paused, then said she would send her son down to pick it up, and would it be possible to wrap the box in something very Chinese, please?

An hour later, a tall, slender young man entered the House of Tong. His hair was yellow, his brows and lashes shades darker, and as he walked past the jades and ancient bronzes, he looked strangely out of place, like a hero dressed in modern clothes performing in a drama of the medieval period. The works of art held a fascination for him, for he continuously looked backward, as if to make certain he had really seen the lovely things that were there. He paused and fixed his eyes on the ancient scroll of calligraphy on the wall directly ahead of him. It held his attention, and with folded arms he continued to look. Fook came over to greet him.

To be in harmony with the studio, Fook, whose voice was normally loud, now spoke English in a soft but emphatic voice, an achievement attained through much practice and effort. His moon-round face beamed with benevolence, the parting in the center of his hair looked sharp and neat. He said, "I see you appreciate calligraphy! Good! It is a most subtle work of art!"

Lin had given Fook some English lessons, and each night in bed he made it a point to learn three long English words before turning out the lights, repeating them over and over again until he fell asleep.

The young man said, his voice gentle, "I'm here to pick up a package for my mother."

"Mrs. Marshall's grandson! You are Mrs. Marshall's grandson! A most per- per- personable-looking young man!" Fook said.

The slender young man extended a hand and said his name was Scott Hayes. Fook took his hand, saying: "I am old enough to be your father. You will call me Mr. Kwong and I shall call you Scott."

Scott said that he too would like to give his grandmother a present and asked the price of a teapot of the Chien Lung period. Fook told him the price. Scott laughed, a gentle laugh. He said he was a college student and could not afford such an amount. His laugh attracted Lin's ears and now she looked up from the account books she was working on. She suggested that he go next door to the Tai Ming Company to select something good but inexpensive. He asked for a suggestion.

She said there were many lovely inexpensive teapots, lacquer boxes, perhaps a box of stationery. He went next door and presently came back to the studio. He showed Lin a large brass bowl which he thought his grandmother could use for her flowers.

"Did I show good judgment?" he asked.

"You showed excellent judgment," Lin answered.

The next evening, Scott came to the studio again, still looking thoroughly out of place among the ancient bronzes and porcelains. He went over to where Lin was. They greeted each other. He said: "My grandmother was very happy with the brass bowl. Of course, it was obvious she was more excited about the brush pot."

"How very nice," Lin said.

She heard the front door open. She excused herself to greet Mrs. Danielson, who had an appointment with Fook to interpret the ancient characters on several seals she had collected. Lin showed Mrs. Danielson to Fook's small office in the studio.

Fook's head was bent low as he studied an old classic on seals. The light shone directly on his head so that it looked like a black lacquer ball, with a white line down the center. At the sight of Mrs. Danielson, he jumped up from his desk, his face beaming with good humor, a hand extended in welcome.

"Mrs. Danielson, I look forward to a most pleasant hour with you. Seals are absolutely fascinating! Lin, please prepare some tea."

"Mrs. Danielson, do you wish cream and sugar?" Lin asked.

"Lin, Lin! Mrs. Danielson will drink tea as we do. Jasmine tea, Mrs. Danielson, I hope jasmine tea pleases you."

Lin left the office to prepare the tea. She was busy with the cups and teapot when Scott came up to her. He said, "Thank you for helping me." She only smiled, for she did not know to what he was referring. He headed for the door. She looked at him for a second and hoped that he had not been offended because she had forgotten about his presence in the studio. She shrugged her shoulders slightly and re-sumed her preparation of the tea.

The next day Scott came again. Over in a corner Lin was busy with her bookkeeping. Fook, ever gracious and cordial, greeted Scott. "Mrs. Marshall's grandson! Good afternoon, Scott. What can I do for you today?"

"Good afternoon, Mr. Kwong. I'm not buying anything today, but if I may, I'd like to look around. These things are all new to me and I find them very beautiful."

"Scott, you are my guest. Stay as long as you wish. What-ever questions you have, ask me."

Fook walked beside Scott, staying with him whenever he stopped at a counter. "That," Scott said, pointing at a pottery piece, "surely that doesn't belong in a Chinese studio."

Fook took the piece out to let Scott examine it more closely.

"A Jewish merchant, Scott! A Tong pottery figure of a Jewish merchant who lived in China during the Tong Dynasty as many foreigners lived in China during that time."

They walked on together. Scott asked, "What is that lovely thing here? It has intrigued me since I first saw it."

"Ah—that object has inspired many dreams for many noblemen and poets—it is a brass opium lamp!"

Fook had an appointment to look at a private collection of porcelains that was being put up for sale. He said to Scott, all his *r*'s sounding like *l*'s: "I am very, very sorry but I must hurry along. I have an engagement. My niece will be very happy to show you around."

Fook left the studio. Scott went over to where Lin was, to say hello. Her greeting was cool for she had been trying to locate a missing receipt. She did not listen to what he

said and found the missing receipt only when he said
goodbye.

The next day Scott was at the studio again. Fook, as
he wiped a lacquer screen, welcomed him. Lin was going
through the mail. Fook was explaining to Scott the many,
many processes of lacquerwork as he continued to wipe
the screen. An invoice puzzled Lin. She waited patiently
as Fook talked on and on. Scott listened with interest,
amazed at the skill of the artisan who had produced the
screen. The sight of Scott, his back to her, annoyed Lin.
She lost her patience, and in a loud voice cried out in
Chinese: "Second Uncle, what is this invoice about? Why
do you bother so much with that white devil boy?"

Fook was obviously displeased. He excused himself and
went over to discuss the invoice with Lin. As Fook talked,
she saw Scott reaching into a glass case to take out a valuable ivory piece. Abruptly she left Fook and walked swiftly
over to Scott. She scolded: "Please do not handle these
things. They are priceless and not for just anyone to
touch!" She took the ivory piece from him in one rough
movement. From across the room, Fook's loud, clear voice
sounded in Chinese: "Why are you so rude to our guest?
There is no harm in touching it! He finds these things
beautiful; your attitude is unworthy!"

It had never ceased to excite Lin to meet someone who
felt a genuine interest in Chinese art. Now she asked herself why had she not felt this way about Scott? Was it because he was so unlike the others, the scholarly-looking
men, or the women who were so soft-spoken, well groomed
and mature. Or was it because he was young and attractive
and, dreading the attraction, she had pretended there was
none and had invented reasons to doubt his interest and
to make him less appealing. Her behavior suddenly became

clear to her and she uttered a rueful little laugh at the realization that she had behaved so stupidly. She said, "Uncle and Mr. Hayes, I'm thoroughly ashamed of myself. Please forgive me."

The ivory piece was still in her hands. She glanced down at it and saw that it was a nude medicine lady. "Let me tell you something about this piece of ivory. In olden days, a wealthy woman, when she was ill, didn't permit a doctor to examine her body. Instead this ivory figure was used to explain to the doctor where the pain was. Though this piece was made for utilitarian purposes, note how delicate the craftsman has made her face, how graceful her legs and thighs. This piece of ivory is yellow with age from four hundred years of existence."

She handed him the piece. He took it, holding it gently, a look of awe on his face.

"It's very lovely," he said. "Won't you continue, and won't you please call me Scott?"

She led him to the tomb pottery figures. "These pieces are my favorites. In very ancient times, when a man died, his wife, his concubines, his servants, his possessions and his animals were buried alive with him so that he could have in the new life the people and things that had been essential to him in the old. In time this practice was denounced and substitutes in pottery for humans and animals were used instead.

"See, here is a three-inch cooking range with a pot; here is a small dressing table complete with toilet boxes and combs. These came from the tomb of some woman who planned to prepare her meals and pamper her appearance in the next life. Here are the clay replicas of a dead man's animals and possessions—a dog, a camel and a chariot."

An hour later there were still more pieces to be shown,

but these, Lin and Scott decided, should be explained another day. He asked her if he could meet her after the studio closed. She said yes, for already she knew that this young man with the gentle voice and ways could become very close to her.

Scott came for Lin at closing time. They decided to go for a walk, crossing over to St. Mary's Square, walking downhill on California Street, arm in arm by the time they were in the quiet, deserted financial section of Montgomery Street. Surrounded by tall buildings of concrete and steel, they talked of ancient art and history.

She told him of the symbolism in flowers, plants and birds; that the plum blossom stands for courage because it is the first to brave the frosts of winters; that the bamboo is like the scholar who is polished and smooth and who, though he may bend in adversity as the bamboo bends before the storm, will not break; that a pair of wild geese flying together symbolizes happy married life because a wild goose takes only one mate.

She told him of the evil Emperor Shih Huang Ti, who reigned from 221 to 210 B.C., who proclaimed himself the First Emperor and ordered all books written before he came into power to be burned so that only his words would be known; the same emperor made slaves of criminals, merchants, and unyielding scholars by forcing them to build the Great Wall of China. The same emperor whose concubines and thousands of slaves were buried alive in his tomb in accordance with his dying wish.

She told him that when he looked at a magnificent monochrome painting he should imagine himself the little figure in the painting meditating among the lofty mountains and winding streams. And as they started uphill back to her home, she promised to let him hold Heaven in his hands in the form of an ancient jade pi.

A few evenings later they had their first dinner together. Lin put aside the fork and knife the waitress had laid out for Scott and took from her handbag two pairs of ivory chopsticks wrapped in blue silk. After they had finished eating and their table was cleared, she took out two pale-blue porcelain cups and out of these they drank chrysanthemum tea sweetened with sugar. A piece of bamboo shoot was on the table. She picked it up and asked Scott if he were aware how good and noble, how old and faithful the bamboo was. Man in China has long used the bamboo to build his home, to shade his rooms, to make chairs and tables. The farmer uses bamboo water pipes to irrigate his land, then carries his crop in woven bamboo baskets hung on each end of a bamboo shoulder pole and walks over suspension bridges slung on bamboo cables to market his products; in the evening, he enjoys music played from wind instruments made from bamboo. Strips of flat bamboo were originally used for writing, which is why the Chinese language is written from top to bottom. Marco Polo, in the thirteenth century, described the summer house of Kublai Khan in Inner Mongolia as being of bamboo cane. A scholar living in the Sung Dynasty wrote that because his home was made of bamboo, the summer shower that came down the roof sounded like the waterfall, and the thick snow of winter sounded like the falling of broken jade.

In the days that followed, the porcelains Lin touched were suddenly more exquisite, the jade pieces more luminous. Each hue in a flower on a painting became more distinct; silk was softer and more luscious to the touch of her hands. Love had come to Lin, and all things of beauty increase in wonder when one is in love.

Lɪɴ ʜᴀᴅ ɪɴᴠɪᴛᴇᴅ Sᴄᴏᴛᴛ ᴛᴏ Sᴜɴᴅᴀʏ ᴅɪɴɴᴇʀ ᴀᴛ ʜᴇʀ ʜᴏᴍᴇ. She said to Fay, "I've invited a Westerner for dinner Sunday. Be sure to make some special dishes."

"Is it Val Beeson?" asked Fay.

"No, but it's a Westerner," answered Lin.

"Now what shall we have," asked Fay, more to herself than to Lin, "bird's nest soup or shark's fin soup?"

Scott arrived, a box of candy in his hand and pleased Fay tremendously when he presented it to her; thus the mildly unpleasant surprise that Lin's guest was a man was assuaged. Fay thanked him in Chinese, for she knew no words of English. As she looked into Scott's eyes her hope was what every mother has in mind when disapproving of a young man who comes to call on her daughter: she can't be serious about him.

Sun was cordial to Scott when they were introduced, for the unpleasant news that their guest was a man had been passed on to him by Fay, who had hurried into the kitchen to tell him. In her haste, she had delivered the following derogatory description to Sun: "Ah! It is a white devil boy!"

Fook appeared from the House of Tong, waving a pottery jug of herb brandy at everyone and jovially warning Scott that he must drink up half the jug.

They sat down to eat, the table resplendent with bowls and spoons in designs of phoenixes and dragons, the generous portions of chicken, duck, greens, and shark's-fin soup assuring them of a long, pleasant meal. Fook poured the herb brandy into small porcelain wine cups: one for Sun, who insisted upon only a few swallows, one for Fay, one for Scott, one for Fook himself, but none for Lin. Then came the invitations to eat, each urging the other on. And from that moment, the talk was endless. Fook described in detail how the food had been prepared. With each swallow of fluffy rice, he took a swallow of herb brandy, filling his wine cup again and again, his round face getting rosier and rosier. Talk never ceased, for much of what was said had to be translated for Fay or for Scott. Fay was in plum-color brocade, and Lin was in peony-pink silk. Scott seemed to like the food and his bowl was never empty, as Fook, in the tradition of a good Chinese host, continued to pick food up for him with the reverse end of his chopsticks. With each swallow of wine, Fook recited a proverb, first in Chinese, then for Scott's benefit in English, making the translation as terse as the Chinese version. Raising his wine cup, a very red-faced Fook said to Scott, "Take wine in large doses; knowledge in small."

"Uncle, the proverb is 'Take knowledge in large doses, wine in small doses,'" corrected Lin.

He looked at her with glowing round eyes. Raising his wine cup again he quoted another proverb, "Fine funerals are assured for parents of good children!"

"What is this talk? What is this talk?" asked Fay.

"Second Uncle is quoting proverbs," Lin answered.

And Fay, herself slightly affected by the herb brandy said, "Second Uncle, quote what you will but remember that my Lin is a maiden."

Said Fook to Fay: "The proverb goes, 'After wine one is without virtue.' But to describe me I compose this, 'Virtue in me remains, though wine in me reigns.'"

Turning to Scott again, he said: "My nephew Kiang, Lin's older brother, loves the proverbs. He studied them, he analyzed them, and he believed in them, for they contain profound wisdom." Taking a generous swallow of herb brandy and assuming a most serious face, Fook resumed: "Here are some of the gems of wisdom most loved by my nephew, somewhere today in the Pacific with the glorious United States Army. Listen: 'Seek a wife for her virtue, a concubine for her beauty.' 'Homely wives and stupid servant girls are more precious than gold.'"

Fook paused for a sip of wine. Sun's lean face was softened by a slight smile, for he too found these old moral maxims absurd in today's world. He cleared his throat, prepared to speak. Because he was extremely sensitive about his limited command of English, Sun spoke it very slowly and whatever he said sounded like the speech of a professor expounding the most profound theory. "'A good cook and a kind heart; a beautiful face and a slender body, a man needs all, so two wives he must have.' Scott, in our village this was often sung in moments of fun; it is an old, old song," Sun said.

Fook, with his wine cup in midair, said: "Do you remember the story of the man who did just that and all the women in the village stoned him because they were afraid their husbands might do the same thing. And the man, bleeding at the forehead, asked what his crime was as he was merely adhering to the saying that a man must have a good cook, a kind heart, a beautiful face, a willowy body, and that therefore he had taken four wives."

When this was translated for Fay, she said: "Ah! These useless men of old! Before I was married I frequently went to my aunt's home. She was the third wife in the house, always walking timidly about, listening like a filial child as her husband warned her, 'A faithful horse will not turn back to eat grass; a faithful wife will not marry a second husband.'"

Fook's face was now a bright red. The jug of wine was empty and he raised it in the air. "Scott, this is my nephew's favorite proverb, 'There is no greater sinner than he who cherishes his wife above his mother and father!'"

Fook lowered the jug to the table, let his head fall on his chest and dozed off to sleep in his chair. Sun and Fay excused themselves. Scott and Lin continued to sit by the kitchen table, Fook deep in intoxicated sleep between them.

Scott said, "I like your family, Lin."

She said, "Thank you, Scott."

A steady muffled snore sounded from Fook. Scott asked, "Why has your uncle never married?"

"He is married, and he has children. Scott, may I tell you about our family?"

"Please do," he said. Lin poured hot jasmine tea into porcelain cups and began to tell Scott the story of the House that Tai Ming Built. Halfway through the story Fook woke up and took over. Sun and Fay came in later and silently joined them. It was close to midnight when Fook concluded, in his accented English, ". . . and Tai Ming was dead at the ven-ne-la-ble age of eighty-seven!"

It was past midnight and once more all were eating. Fook had somehow found chicken chow mein and jumbo fried prawns that they dipped in tomato sauce. Much talking, much laughing, and much joking again. Sun was polite and sober, Fook was loud and drinking herb brandy again, and Scott was suddenly having a great deal of difficulty with his chopsticks and noodles. They were all happy that evening.

ONE CLEAR SATURDAY NOON, THROUGH A NARROW SIDE street, Lin and Scott walked arm in arm. Winding through the air, a shrill melody from the strings of a butterfly harp rose from one of the many high-balconied homes. Scott and Lin walked leisurely on the unpaved street on their way to an old temple, erected to serve the religious souls of the Sons of Tong of San Francisco.

This side street that escaped the eyes of tourists was the replica of a street that the Sons of Tong had known before they crossed the Pacific Ocean: balcony rose upon balcony on buildings as close together as two coats of vermilion lacquer upon a folding screen; gilded hardwood banners, the names of family or guild associations stiffly painted upon them, hung above the curved tiled roofs; sharp noises all about told that the mah-jongg pieces were being "washed" and that many series of East, South, West and North would be played, and it would be the following day before the games were finally over.

On the floors of the many balconies, in the windows of

the shops, at the foot of a shaky stairway leading up to a crowded domicile, were touching signs of the love of pretty things: tall green plants sprawling beyond the rim of a wooden tub; gay artificial flowers in gaudy vases; a clever paper snake made by the nimble fingers of a craftsman in Canton, swaying to and fro in front of a porcelain Laughing Buddha. Coming out of his small shop was the town's oldest carpenter, carrying a bucket of water and a water pipe, ready for a pleasant afternoon as he sat in a battered rattan chair to smoke in the warm sun. He was framed against a background of his own design, a door decorated with odd pieces of tile, ironwork and wood carvings salvaged from his various contracting jobs. He raised a hand to greet Lin. Lin reciprocated, thinking how Val would have liked to sketch him now against his odd-looking door, with his wispy gray hair and the lines on his face so deep they might have been engraved by his own working tools.

Children surrounded Scott and Lin as they walked, some regarding them unabashed but most of them shy. The girls wore straight fringes of hair across their foreheads, the boys' hair had been trimmed by following the contours of a round porcelain bowl upon their small heads. One very tiny boy was allowed the freedom his mother and father had enjoyed when they were little in their village home in the Hills of Tong. Dressed only in a warm sweater and brown sandals, he passed his water whenever and wherever he pleased. One little girl boldly tugged at Lin's emerald-green silk sheath to get her attention. She inquired in Chinese, for she was a child of preschool age: "Why are you with this man? He's not a Son of Tong. He has yellow hair. I've never seen one of us and a yellow-hair together."

Lin replied, "He's a Westerner, a good friend of mine.

I'm taking him to the Temple of the God of Wealth."

"Why?" she demanded to know.

"He's never seen the temple before. He wants to see it."

A little boy, holding a piece of moist, hot ginger in his soiled hand as once Lin used to do, called out loudly, "He's very tall!"

One little girl remarked to another little girl: "Do you think the lady is pretty?" In all seriousness the little girl answered: "Yes, but wouldn't she be prettier if her hair were curly?"

Another child cried out, "His eyes are blue!" only to wound Lin ever so slightly as she heard the high, giggling voice conclude, "how funny that is!"

Lin turned to Scott, who had been looking on in friendly interest. She said: "Scott, don't you think these children are absolutely enchanting? But do you mind ever so much that they think your blue eyes are funny?" His head tilted back in gentle laughter and the children joined him in a louder chorus. He stooped to the ground and became the height of the tallest child in the group. He said: "Now you wonderful children don't really think my eyes are funny, do you? Of course I wish mine were chocolate brown like yours, but it's not my luck."

The children did not understand him and one child asked, "What did the man say?" Lin told her, her eyes on Scott as she talked, for the sun had made his hair a golden yellow, a shade she had seen once before on the silk-embroidered wings of a delicate butterfly on a robe of the Ching Dynasty. Scott got up and Lin took his arm and together they walked on. The band of children scattered. Already they had lost interest in the couple and their attention now turned to a black cat sunning himself in the street.

Lin and Scott paused in front of the old temple. Scott opened the red door and they went inside. The fragrance from sandalwood joss sticks and red candles was pleasantly strong; from years of daily burning the smell had permeated the very pores of the building. Above them was a large paper lantern; the bottom just touched Scott's head; the lighting was dim, and the quiet gave such an air of solemnity that Scott and Lin walked up the long narrow flight of stairs without speaking a word. They reached the top and were greeted by the Earth God, of whom they asked permission to enter.

When they came to the God of Wealth, Scott and Lin stopped. The god was gilded and painted, and before him were the offerings of good food and wine of the faithful. On either side of the elaborate altar were the god's weapons—the wooden spears and swords required to fight evil spirits. Upon the floor were red silk pillows bearing the marks of hundreds of religious souls who had knelt on them to intone for favors. Sandalwood joss sticks and red candles stood upon mounds of sand in huge brass burners. Wooden plaques bearing complimentary inscriptions hung all around, the gifts of grateful worshipers whose prayers had been answered. The dancing light from tens of slim red candles, from burning wicks upon old copper dishes played upon the gilt and colors of the God of Wealth and the winding smoke seemed to be his very breath.

The old caretaker of the temple shuffled past in his black cotton slippers and nodded to them. In the dim light Scott's hair no longer looked golden; it was pale yellow. Scott asked, "Can you worship this God of Wealth and worship the God of Medicine also?"

Lin answered, "These gods are not jealous gods. They ask only that the heart be true."

He looked at her, the flame from a red candle lighting the lower half of his face. He said, "Only that the heart be true." He paused, and with a slight hint of urgency in his voice, said, "Lin, there's something I'd like you to know." But they were not alone, for an old woman had entered the temple. She walked past them as if they were not there, moving softly and slowly on her bound feet. She lit a joss stick, placed it on the mound of sand, knelt on the red pillow and kowtowed to the God of Wealth. They watched her as she softly chanted a prayer, her hands folded and her eyes closed, an earnest expression on her wrinkled face. Lin motioned Scott to follow her, and holding hands they went in search of a place to talk.

In the room of the fortuneteller Scott told Lin: "All the men on both sides of our family have been doctors—both my grandfathers and my father. Since I was a little boy, there were constant daily reminders that I was to be a doctor too. My mother, my father, my grandparents always took it for granted that I would practice medicine. So I grew up with that idea; it was an idea accepted without any questioning or any thought of questioning on my side. Then I went to college. I did well in my first year but in the beginning of my second year I began to wonder: am I going to be a doctor because I want to, because I'm interested, because I really want to, or am I going into this because I've been told to go into it, because I haven't given myself the time and the opportunity to think of going into something else. I had to find out.

"I told my mother my problem but she couldn't understand. She simply insisted that medicine was for me. I decided that the answer could be arrived at only within myself. I dropped out of school and I left San Francisco. I had absolutely no idea where I was going or what I was going to do. All I knew was that I had to go away, to be away from everyone I knew. I traveled all over the country; the Middle West, the South, the New England States. I traveled in all sorts of ways. I hitchhiked, I rode on trains and buses when I could pay, I even hopped freight trains. I did all kinds of manual work on farms. At nights I asked myself: Would I like to build bridges, or fix carburetors, or grow cabbages, or fly a plane, or run a grocery store or take up law. In half a year's time, I realized I really wanted to go into medicine, that I wanted to diagnose and treat and cure. I wanted to go into it because I was really interested in it, not because my family had been in it, or because I had been told and expected to go into it."

"Your heart was true," Lin said.

The caretaker, who was also the fortuneteller, shuffled into the room. Behind him was a woman. The two of them went to a corner desk. The woman was given a set of bamboo sticks in a box and holding the box with both hands she shook it vigorously until one stick dropped out.

"Yes, my heart was true," Scott said.

The fortuneteller read out the inscribed number on the stick and checked the corresponding number in a soft-cover book that contained the fortunes.

"Thank you for telling me all this, Scott," Lin said, wishing they were alone.

"Ah—your outlook is bright! very bright. . . ." Lin heard the thin voice of the fortuneteller telling the woman. "Ah . . ." the woman sighed in deep gratitude.

"And Lin, when I came back to San Francisco, it was as if I were seeing the city for the first time," said Scott.

The room was small. The woman turned and looked at them, silently imploring Scott and Lin with her eyes to be quiet for just a little while as her very bright future was told her.

Lin said in Chinese, "I'm sorry."

The woman smiled and said, "You are very kind."

"Ah," began the fortuneteller again, "all lawsuits are in your favor. There will be no serious illnesses in the family. An important letter bearing happy news is due soon. In matters of which you are ignorant, do not mingle and there will be no difficulties. There is something in your heart very dear and important to you. Be patient concerning this. The time for its arrival is due soon."

"Ah—good, good," sighed the woman, gratefully tendering a dollar bill to the old man upon her departure.

"Scott, go on with what you were saying," Lin urged.

"I never knew there was so much to this city," he began.

The fortuneteller was looking at Lin; he interrupted, "Are you not the Kwong girl of the Tai Ming Company?"

She nodded.

He came up close to Scott and Lin. "Would this Westerner like his fortune told? Ah—for the two of you I will charge a cheaper price. Would you like to?"

But Lin shook her head. "Come, Scott, let's go somewhere where we can talk."

They left the Temple of the God of Wealth, and on their way out, Lin gave thanks to the Earth God for having given them permission to enter. They walked down the dark stairway, the good fragrance of the sandalwood joss sticks descending with them.

LATER THAT SAME EVENING, AFTER THE CLOSING OF THE studio, Lin took Scott to the Chinese theater. They stood among the crowd waiting to buy their tickets, hearing continuous talk and shrill laughter from every man, woman and child, Scott's yellow hair conspicuous among the sleek black heads surrounding them.

It had been many years since Lin had been in this theater. As her world had extended beyond the boundaries of the Chinese quarters she had come to know and love and prefer Beethoven and Chopin, Cole Porter and George Gershwin.

Scott and Lin sat in the center row, between a young mother with a baby in her arms and an old woman dressed in a loose black jacket and trousers. The mood of the audience was relaxed and informal. It was as Lin remembered it in her childhood. There were the children, dozens and dozens of them, running up and down the aisle, crowding before the stage, bumping against legs and knees as they pushed through a row of seats to get to their parents to beg for a nickel for a treat.

There was the constant eating of melon seeds, of coconut strips, of hot ginger, of lichee nuts, of pickled apricots. There were the constant cries of babies in the arms of young mothers who would thrust pacifiers in their infants' mouths so that they could go on blissfully enjoying the play. There was the loud greeting of one woman high in the balcony to a woman down below. There was the constant talking, loud and ceaseless, whether the actors and actresses were on or off the stage.

There was the hysterical laughter from the audience when the cardboard tree the propman was about to put on the stage fell from his hands and landed on his small feet. There was the kind applause from the audience for the hero; the sighs for the beautiful heroine; the unmerciful laughter for the villain. There was the beat, beat, beat of the drum, the clash of golden cymbals, the whining vibration of a violin. The story of Lady Precious Stream began.

The time was the Tong Dynasty, and gathered in Premier Wong's beautiful garden were his large family and friends. It was winter, the season of the plum blossom. Enter Lady Precious Stream, the beautiful third daughter of Premier Wong, who kowtows to her parents for arriving late. Premier Wong suddenly requests a large stone table on which his family and guests may compose poems. Servants are ordered to carry the table from the garden to the veranda. Four servants are unable to move the stone table. Premier Wong's two sons-in-law are unable to lift it and feel humiliated.

Enter Pingkwe, a young servant, who lifts the table with ease and sets it on the veranda. Family and friends now compose clever poems and recite them. It was the elder son-in-law's turn to recite his poem, but with embarrassment he confesses he has been unable to write one. To avert attention from his failure, he turns to Pingkwe and asks him to compose a verse. To everyone's surprise the young servant composes a beautiful poem. This angers the elder son-in-law and the party breaks up.

It is the next day and Premier Wong is discussing with Lady Precious Stream the choice of a husband for her. Lady Precious Stream insists that she will not marry a man of the type of her two brothers-in-law, who are wealthy but pompous and incapable of noble deeds. Father and daughter agree to leave the matter of the man to fate; they would set a day when she would throw out a bouquet of flowers from a balcony and whoever caught it, rich or poor, brilliant or dull, would be her future husband.

The day arrives and men from all parts of the country gather below the balcony, anxiously awaiting the tossing of the bouquet. In the servants' quarter, the cooks tease Pingkwe about going outside to catch the bouquet. Finally Pingkwe says he will go, but only to humor them.

Up in the balcony, Lady Precious Stream notices Pingkwe and throws the bouquet in his direction. The handsome young servant catches it. But alas, Premier Wong will not consent to the marriage. Pingkwe rebukes Premier Wong for his breach of promise, as does Lady Precious Stream. Father and daughter clap hands three times to show that each has disowned the other.

So Lady Precious Stream follows the young servant and in a simple ceremony in a humble hut the two are wed.

Then Pingkwe tells Lady Precious Stream that he is in fact Prince Lee Wen, the son of the emperor. He shows her his golden seal and confides to her that his mother had been killed by a jealous concubine and that afterward he had been sold to a poor family.

One morning, on his way to the city to sell his firewood, Pingkwe comes across a notice posted on a wall calling for men to fight the invading Tartars. He immediately goes to join the army, but the two commanders of this army are Lady Precious Stream's pompous brothers-in-law. They make a condition whereby Pingkwe can join the army only if he can succeed in taming a wild red horse. But Pingkwe is brave and strong and succeeds in taming the horse, and is given command of the vanguard.

Pingkwe returns home and tells Lady Precious Stream that he is now commander of an army. She weeps and waves farewell to him as he answers the call of the drums.

Into battle Pingkwe goes, riding alongside the brothers-in-law. But, unknown to him, the two still hate him and are plotting to kill him. One evening they offer him a glass of wine with cocaine in it. Pingkwe becomes unconscious and is tied to a swift horse that runs wildly among the Tartars' tents.

Upon regaining consciousness, Pingkwe finds himself in front of the Tartar king. Also present is Princess Tai-Sen. She intervenes on his behalf, and instead of being killed he is taken to the water dungeon. The next day Princess Tai-Sen asks Pingkwe to join the Tartars. This the former servant steadfastly refuses to do. Again and again she pleads, and again and again he refuses until in anger he throws himself upon the cot. Just then, unknown to him, his golden seal falls to the ground. Princess Tai-Sen picks up the seal and leaves the dungeon. Outside the prison, she examines the seal and realizes that Pingkwe is the son of the emperor. So now the Princess plots to marry him.

Eighteen years have passed and Lady Precious Stream now considers herself a widow. Pingkwe is still in the water dungeon. The Princess Tai-Sen is now a queen. She still desires Pingkwe. So she requests a captured Chinese general to bring the golden seal to Pingkwe and ask that they be united in marriage. But the captured general is loyal to his own people and propounds a scheme to Pingkwe to falsely consent to the marriage in order to secure his freedom. Pingkwe agrees and is freed from the water dungeon. Together he and the general conspire to attack the Tartars from within the city, for they have received secret news that the Chinese army is nearing the Tartar capital. When the Chinese army arrives, Pingkwe clears their way into the palace and thus the Tartars are conquered. In her chambers, heartbroken that Pingkwe has betrayed her, the Queen plunges a glittering sword into her slender white throat and dies.

Upon a swift horse Pingkwe gallops back to his humble hut, to his Lady Precious Stream. Later he presents his golden seal to his father the emperor, and father and son are happily united. Upon the emperor's retirement, Pingkwe becomes the ruling monarch. As emperor, he issues orders to arrest the two brothers-in-law who had tried to kill him. He sentences them to death, but Lady Precious Stream begs Pingkwe to forgive the past and spare her brothers-in-law. This Pingkwe does. So the story ends with the whole family reunited and "the chastity and faithfulness of Lady Precious Stream lived forever."

As the performance went on, Scott and Lin gradually joined the pleasures of the crowd as they chewed melon seeds and ate pickled apricots and coconut strips. Shortly after Pingkwe had caught Lady Precious Stream's bouquet of flowers, two little girls with sticky hands and mouth joined their mother who sat with a baby in her arms next to Lin and Scott. Their dark, almond-shaped eyes under straight fringes of hair stared shyly at Scott and Lin until he offered them the remains of their bag of coconut strips. Then the younger one, with cheeks as pink as the petals of a peony, climbed onto Lin's lap and put her head against Lin's breast and fell asleep.

Throughout the entire performance there was never a scene without breathtakingly beautiful costumes in crimson, purple, Imperial yellow, emerald green and turquoise, all of them trimmed with sparkling sequins, bright beads and silk tassels, and made by the patient hands of consummate artists in China. Lin especially admired a headdress studded with pearls, brilliants, and artificial flowers on the heroine with skin like *blanc-de-chine,* although Scott insisted that the long, sweeping pheasant plumes on the headdress of a general were more impressive.

It was well past midnight when the performance was over and Lin and Scott were outside in the street. Fathers holding the hands of sleepy children, and mothers holding sleeping babies in their arms passed them, hurrying in the chilly midnight to get home. Scott and Lin, arms linked together, walked slowly and turned a corner toward a restaurant for fried won ton.

IN ACCORDANCE WITH THE ANCIENT PRINCIPLE OF THE Yin and the Yang, a Chinese proverb goes: "When a flower is in full bloom, it soon wilts; when blossoms are in abundance, they soon fall; when a wine cup is full, it must overflow." Surely the happiness that filled Lin in her love for Scott must have reached its limit the day her father Sun called her into his office.

He bade her sit down, saying it would take him only a few minutes to finish his business. He was completing the monthly task of sending money home to the House that Tai Ming Built. Money would be cabled through the Bank of China in New York to Chungking and from Chungking south. There was now no other means of communication overseas.

Lin sat opposite him. Behind him on the wall was a family portrait taken shortly before Grandfather Kwong left San Francisco. He sat in the center, erect, his face unsmiling and stern. Sun and Fay were on either side of him, Sun's hair already gray, and young Kiang sat by his side. In the portrait Lin herself stood by Fay and she remembered that the photographer had said the portrait was spoiled because she had sucked her thumb just as the picture was snapped. However, Grandfather Kwong had insisted that the portrait was very good. Now Grandfather Kwong was an invalid; he had never recovered from his fall when the family had fled to the hills. Gradually his health had worsened. His last letter to Lin was hardly legible; it had been brief and it had ended, ". . . your old grandfather's hands are now useless; they are not in harmony with my mind and heart that still think of you."

She remained quiet and waited until Sun was through. The round, happy face of Fook never failed to cheer her; the long, dignified face of Sun with his gray hair and staid composure always prompted Lin's most filial behavior. Sun now reached for the abacus and, after verifying some figures, he looked up.

He inquired softly: "Lin, have you been seeing this Westerner, Scott, every day?"

"Yes," she replied.

Obviously taken aback, he said, "Lin, certainly you are not serious about this Westerner."

"I'm very fond of Scott," she said.

Sun's face began to show anger and harshly he said: "This cannot be! This cannot be! You must not see him anymore. I myself was not aware that you had been seeing him so much. Do you wish to know how I found out? People are talking! Twice today I heard people gossiping about the Kwong girl of the Tai Ming Company and a white devil boy. You had the audacity to take him to the temple last week. Is that true?"

"Yes, I took him last Saturday. Father, what objections

do you have to Scott? You've met him. Isn't he a fine person?"

He sighed deeply. "Lin, when he came up to our house for dinner I assumed he was someone you went to the university with for always some of your or Kiang's college friends have come to the house. Never for a moment did I think that an affair such as what has been going on would come of it. Certainly he is a fine person; that I know from talking to him, but to see him every day, to walk through town arm in arm as if . . . this I will not allow a daughter of mine to do!"

In a rare moment of uncontrolled anger, she cried out: "Father, you have no right to speak to me like this! You have no right to forbid me to see Scott!"

As quickly as the words had rushed out, she realized she should never have said them. How well she knew that he had every right to tell her what to do, what to say, and how to act as long as she was a daughter in the home. Sun struck an angry fist upon the desk; the beads on the abacus clicked. He said: "Indeed you are an unworthy daughter, void of any filial devotion. You will see no more of this person. To say the least, it is an impossible situation!"

He left the room and Lin sat alone in the small office. She stared at the picture across from her. She did not like the picture of Grandfather Kwong, for no benevolence showed in his face; his eyes were stern and his mouth rigid, he whom she remembered as always good and kind to her. She felt the need to talk. She said out loud to him: "Scott is white, I am not; is that a reason for Father to object to our being in love?"

She rose from her chair and headed for the door. She paused, for she guessed the answer Grandfather would give. She turned her head and looked at him again. Then, with the faintest trace of anger, for she dared not show more, she spoke, "We in the Chinese quarter cry out against racial intolerance when we feel discriminated against; what should we call it when we ourselves do not look beyond the color of the skin?"

She walked over to the wall and faced Grandfather Kwong. She could almost hear him calling her unfilial: she had committed the cardinal sin of speaking back to her elders. In a family such as theirs, in moments of reproof the rule was, think what you may but hold your tongue. Now she was sure she heard those exact words from him, and because he was only black and white and flat upon the wall she slapped her hands in anger and cried to him: "Filial piety! Filial piety! That is all one hears in this family." But in another second she said softly, "I'm sorry." She repeated again, "I'm sorry." She took one final look at him to see if he understood, for her mind was made up. She would continue to see Scott.

She left the small office and hurried out into the street. She knew Scott was on his way to the studio. She saw him as he was about to cross and motioned him to stay where he was. She joined him and together they went to the park. She told him all that had happened and what her feelings were. She caught the look of surprise on his face, and for a brief moment she wondered if it were there not so much that a family had objected to him as that a Chinese family had. Her heart had not been at ease, and now the pain was greater still. She knew that if she asked him the reason for the look, whatever the answer was, these would be the last words she would ever hear from him.

FAY'S HANDS WERE TAUT; ONE OF THEM CLUTCHED THE
ends of her long straight hair, the other gripped a small,
narrow brush. Her hands were slightly rough for she had
spent a great deal of time washing her hair which fell to
her waist when it was undone. It took several hours in the
sun to dry her hair and it had been almost dry when Sun
had entered the bedroom to talk to her. Now she sat on a
stool looking up at him, her hair and back to the stream
of sun slanting in; he stood by the bed where there was
no sun.

The moment he had come into the room, Fay had
known that a matter of importance was on his mind. It
was unusual for him to come back to the house during the
day except when it was time for his noon meal. He had
come in looking half-apologetic and his greeting had been,
"You are drying your hair?"

She had smiled, for she welcomed his unexpected presence and had replied, "Yes, it is so warm and restful in the
sun."

She noticed the look of deep concern on his serious face and how restless he was as she waited for him to speak. Then she said: "Sun, why don't you sit down? This is a matter of importance; is it so or is it not so?"

He sat on the bed and he had to look downward to speak to her. He asked her if she remembered Scott; did she know that Lin was serious about him and that he had warned her she must see no more of him? He repeated, almost word for word, the conversation between Lin and himself in his office.

She listened, brushing out her hair as she did, a hand gripping and tugging at the roots when a point in his talk distressed her. When he told her how Lin had rebuked him, her hand knocked against the pottery jar full of wood shavings soaking in water which she used to make the lacquer for her hair.

When he had finished they were both silent, each deep in private thoughts about the same problem. Fay was a portrait waiting for a Western painter. The dark green sash of the window framed her against a background of soft daylight. Her head slanted downward. Her black hair sprang in abundance from her high forehead, and fell in heavy lines away from her tilted head. Only one small jade earring showed. Her eyes were not deep-set, so that her long lashes were straight. The pupils were black, the iris dark brown and nowhere did her maturity and strength show more clearly than in her large, steady eyes.

He had come to her for a solution, she knew, and now he waited for her to speak. But to her distress, she had no solution, knowing only that if she had she would have presented it to him. He would then think her words over and present it in his own words as if he had thought it up. She would then agree, not saying that it had been her idea;

how well she knew that a man liked to think himself the master of the house!

Her perplexed gaze was toward the floor but Sun's eyes were on her. For a few brief moments his thoughts were not of his child but of his wife, thinking: truly she grows lovelier with maturity.

She turned her head and looked at him, unsmiling. In her voice with the tones of a jade bell she said: "I will talk to her. We will come to an understanding."

He felt a surge of relief and now as only in moments of complete honesty he made the rare admission to himself that indeed she knew and controlled their children better than he.

Her hair was now completely dry. She dipped the narrow brush into the pottery jar of lacquer, and brushed it to her forehead, catching the drippings with a quick hand. She would continue to brush it, beginning from the roots down to the uneven ends until each strand of straight hair was smooth and shiny. Now it was completely lacquered and the heavy texture of her hair gave it a look of fine brocade.

She started to coil her hair. She had been aware that Sun's eyes had been on her all this time. Now she looked up and caught his expression and she knew that he did not know the kindness in his face. Often at night before she went to bed he stood behind her while she combed out her hair at the dressing table. In the small mirror she would see his face, not stern then, but as it now was. Then when the lights were out and they were both in bed his hand would reach out to her. Fumbling, he would loosen the drawstring of her trousers. He would stroke her stomach; then his hand would reach down to her thigh and over and over he would stroke it there. And then it was her secret that this man who to the world seemed the sternest of moralists was possessed of intense passion, a passion that even now had not abated; a passion that was never hers.

Now she called his name so that the word spoken in the silence would remind him that it was not evening. He immediately became self-conscious again and his expression even sterner than usual. She hoped she had not wounded his feelings. She continued to coil her hair, her eyes on him.

He cleared his throat and started to leave the room. She called out: "Sun, it is almost time for lunch. You may as well stay up here. Early this morning I had a yearning for soup noodles so that I had all the ingredients prepared before I washed my hair. If you would boil the water now it will not be long before we eat."

He said softly, "Ah! Soup noodles! Good! I will boil the water now."

She said, as she reached for a jade hairpin: "You will need to fill the whole kettle."

His hand was on the doorknob, his face turned to her. He said, his expression no longer self-consciously stern, "That will be done."

LIN AND FAY, SO ALIKE IN FIGURE AND THE DELICACY OF their features, sat near each other in the latter's bedroom where the generous sun shone in. Lin wore a loose-fitting red brocade jacket, a black décolleté dress, and a single strand of cultured pearls; Fay wore a Chinese dress of light-weight wool in celadon green with a high collar, jade ear-rings, and a jade heart hung from a gold chain at her throat.

The sunlight shone on the brilliant hair of both mother and daughter, for Lin had inherited the thick, lustrous hair of her mother. Fay's chignon was larger and more beautiful, for her hair was longer. In a drawer was a chignon Fay had once used when her own hair had been shorter, made from the hair of an enterprising Son of Tong who had sold his queue that he had cut off after the over-throw of the Manchus; many other Sons of Tong had been equally enterprising.

Lin's choice of coloring in cosmetics was vivid; Fay preferred subdued tones and her lips, colored by blotting them with red paper, bore no well defined outline as did Lin's.

For the past half hour Fay had listened attentively as Lin talked about Scott and herself. Lin talked willingly and freely, at times defiantly, for she felt herself on the defensive, and only changed to a more agreeable tone when she saw that Fay's attitude was totally sympathetic.

At first Fay was amused by her daughter's air of independence as Lin continued to assert her freedom to choose her friends. Then amusement turned to mild envy as Fay recalled her own youth when she had had no choice but to accept the man chosen for her in marriage. It was not romance Fay envied, however, it was the independent spirit of her daughter, that Fay herself had not had until she was the mother of two school-age children. But envy was quickly gone as she heard her daughter say hotly, "Father has no right to forbid me to see him!" for Fay concluded that independence in the young was much too mixed with arrogance.

"Lin, you will not shout so again."

"But Father's attitude is so intolerable!"

"Lin, I asked you not to shout so."

"But it's true!"

A hand went up to Fay's eyes as she closed them; the other hand beckoned Lin not to speak. What had it been like when she herself was young in the Hills of Tong? Never had she raised her voice to her mother or father; never had it been necessary for them to ask her not to raise her voice to them; never had Sun or Fook ever raised their voices in anger to speak to Grandfather Kwong. She opened her eyes again when she heard Lin ask if she wished a cup of tea.

"I don't want any tea now," she said, knowing the gesture was meant for an apology.

"Lin, it is for your own good that we wish you to see no more of this Westerner."

"But why?"

"The affair has only begun. If it continues it will be more difficult; the attachment may become stronger."

Lin rose from her chair and walked to the window. She kept her eyes on the view across the street, the rolling green lawn of the park. Fay looked at her daughter whom she could see in profile. Once in the Hills of Tong, she herself had stood thus by a window after learning she was to be married. She had had implicit faith in her parents' choice and the years had proved her trust in them to be right. The years with Sun had been good and not only with Sun but with Sun's people. Even now in the Hills of Tong her people and Sun's people continued friendly relations, remembering each other with gifts at the time of the New Year.

"Don't allow the attachment to become stronger. End it now," she repeated.

Lin continued to stare out of the window. Fay remained patient, for the problem was delicate. She looked at Lin's red jacket and it brought back memories of her wedding when she had worn the same jacket for the first time. What an elaborate affair it had been, with days of celebration before and after the ceremony; it had been a time to be ostentatious. At her home before the wedding, gifts of food and jewelry from Sun's family had arrived. In turn, her own family had made gifts to Sun's family. After the wedding ceremony she and Sun had knelt before senior relatives who had taken turns in sitting down to accept tea offered by the bride and groom. After the third day of the wedding she and Sun had returned to her parents' home for an elaborate noon meal, still as part of the ceremonies.

She called to Lin to return to the chair near hers. She placed a hand on her daughter's shoulder and said, "You will promise to see no more of him."

"I can't," she said.

"What could it lead to? Certainly you can't think of marriage with this person."

"Why not?" Lin asked quietly.

Fay's hands grew tense. "Because marriage is an affair between two families. It is not merely a relationship between husband and wife, it is the relationship of a wife to her husband's father, mother, brothers and sisters and also a harmonious relationship between parents of both sides. With a Westerner, how could this be possible when neither I nor your father will ever know him or his people?"

"This affair is between Scott and myself."

It was an angry Fay who now spoke, no longer in tones of a jade bell: "Have all my words been spoken for nothing! Have you no ears for reason?" She rose from her chair and stood by the window until her anger wore off. Then she returned to her chair. "Lin, if I haven't made you understand my reasons, will you ask further?" She looked at Lin with undivided attention, waiting in good faith for her to speak.

"Let me go away for a few days to decide what to do," Lin said.

"Where would you go?"

"I'll go to Val's place. I'll stay for several days to think this thing over."

This was something entirely alien to Fay. That an unmarried daughter would leave her home to go to another's was almost unthinkable. Her voice was angry again. "You will not go to Val's home. We will come to an agreement now. You will promise not to see this Westerner again."

Lin got up and, without saying a word, left the room. Fay remained in her chair, feeling angry, hurt and helpless. Now she wondered if her angry words had been wise; she would go to Lin and they would talk again. She poured herself a cup of tea and drank it slowly, thinking of what she should probably say to her daughter.

She left her room and met Lin in the hallway, dressed in a coat, an overnight suitcase in her hand.

"Lin, where are you going?"

"I'm going to stay with Val."

"No, don't rush out to others when you have us."

"I'll stay only a few days."

"Lin! You will agree to nothing I ask! I would strike you if it would do any good! But what can force do that reason cannot!"

Lin hurried down the stairs. She went to the studio for her purse. Fook approached her, guessing what had happened. She was in no mood to talk, not even to her beloved uncle. She brushed past him and said without looking at him: "Val's phone number is in my drawer. Give it to Scott when he calls. I'll be at her home for several days."

She left the studio. Fook watched her as she crossed the street to take the cable car down to the Ferry Building. His fingers stroked the tiny jade tiger he wore looped on his belt. He shook his head sadly, for he was more aware of the ways of the West and Westerners than either Sun or Fay. He said aloud for all the gods and goddesses of ivory to hear: "She will be hurt. Our Lin will be deeply hurt."

VAL BEESON'S HEAD WAS LARGE AND ROUND, HER FACE a perfect circle. Her skin was very light, the color very even; the texture was good, and up close one could see that it was covered with a delicate fuzz like a peach. She was a tall girl with an abundance of flesh and muscle distributed in even proportion throughout.

Her hair was blond but thin and fine, so that no matter how carefully she arranged it, it soon took on a disordered look. She darkened her light brows and lashes with soft brown pencil to give her face character. She had difficulty finding clothes because of her size, and often wore a man's shirt and woman's jeans at home and walked about barefoot to save her expensive extra large shoes. But in spite of dirty jeans, paint-streaked shirts and untidy hair, Val never looked dirty because of her extremely fair, healthy coloring.

To Val's small cottage across the bay in Berkeley, Lin had gone for refuge, climbing a long flight of terrazzo steps, passing a large Swiss-chalet-type house to get to Val's cottage in the rear.

[188]

The front door opened immediately into the living room of this small cottage and the pine-wood floor was bare. There was a fireplace, and nearby against the wall, books and magazines were stacked unevenly. Only when the nights were hot did the fireplace go unused and lately, since the nights had alternated between warm and cool, it had been used every evening.

A visitor could tell where Val was accustomed to sit on the floor in front of the fire, although no pillows or chairs were nearby. A long, seemingly permanent trail of cigarette ash led to a clear-red ceramic ashtray a few feet from the fireplace; where the ashes began, Val would sit, her ample posterior needing no pillow.

Prints, large and small, predominantly of the French impressionists and several oil and charcoal works of Val's covered the walls, tacked from ceiling to base. All three walls were so decorated; a narrow window ran almost the whole width of the fourth wall, ending at the door that led out to a tiny veranda facing a wall of fragrant leaves.

The living room was small, the bedroom smaller yet and throughout the apartment everything was always, like Val herself, in attractive disarray.

Two days ago Lin had taken the train to Berkeley to Val's cottage, waiting on the terrazzo steps until Val came home from work. Val had rushed to greet her and had hugged her like a mother cat her kitten. Lin had said, "Val, I'll talk later; just let me stay a day or two with you."

And Val had replied, as she picked up Lin's suitcase, "I'm seething with curiosity, but I'll ask questions only after you start talking."

Val had taken two days off from her work as a commercial artist to stay with Lin. They had been spent with oil paints and canvas on a hill; in the evening they sat on a couch pulled from a corner to face the fireplace. The first night Lin had said virtually nothing. Sensing her unhappiness, Val had held her peace and had kept busy repairing a folding canvas chair she used for outdoor painting. This unusual silence caused no discomfort between them.

The second night, while a fire blazed, Lin told Val the reason for her flight. The small living room was lighted only by the glow of the burning wood. Lin concluded: "Val, I don't want to break with my family, but I don't want to give Scott up. What do you think, Val, does it look hopeless?"

Val, looking extremely serious, said, "I wish I could tell you what to do; I very much wish I could!"

They talked on and on in front of the fire. Val constantly reminded Lin of the strong unity in their family; repeatedly Lin retorted that she could never give up Scott.

To Val, Lin's family was a rare and enviable one and again and again she compared it with her own family life, so shaken by divorce and remarriage.

"I spent all the school months with my father and stepmother, all the vacation months with my mother and stepfather, most of the time wishing I didn't have to spend time with any of them. But there's such a marvelous cohesiveness in your family. Don't give them up."

Fresh firewood had just been tossed into the fire; it was blazing again. Lin looked at Val as she talked, her full face slightly flushed from the warmth. To Lin, Val's soft cheeks looked like two cupcakes frosted with fresh pink icing, and on the heels of such a pleasant thought came an ugly one that Val might really object to the relationship because Scott was white and she was not. Instantly she regretted it, and reached for Val's hand and said, "Val Beeson, you're a dear friend."

Val patted Lin's hand affectionately. "Lin Kwong, I love you too. Now shall we get ready for bed?"

Val got up from the couch, stretching her arms and legs, looking tremendous from where Lin saw her. Lin put her legs up and stretched out on the couch. She closed her eyes and thought of Scott.

Val said, "Lin Kwong, I said, shall we get ready for bed?"

Half in dreams, Lin said: "Lin Kwong . . . Lin Kwong . . . Lin Kwong. . . . I wish I had been born an O'Malley, or a Smith."

Val exploded: "What utter nonsense! You know you don't mean that! O'Malley! Smith! Really!"

Lin sat up on the sofa. She saw on the wall a silhouette of Val in profile, looking like a fairy-tale giant as she tilted her head to blow smoke rings in the air. Lin asked, "Val, how would you like Lin Baccigaluppi?"

On the third day Lin was alone in the cottage. Val had returned to work. She was lonely and unhappy and she missed the House of Tong. She missed the feel of ivory, of porcelain, of jade; she missed the romantic imaginings that stirred in her whenever she handled precious things. Every morning when she woke up she was greeted by a still life of a dead fish on a silver platter. She wanted to see life and movement again in paintings, to see winding streams, bamboos in the wind, beautiful children at play, proud birds in flight.

Gone was the novelty of cooking alone, as she unskillfully handled frying pan and coffeepot. She went out to the small veranda to eat, but even air and sunshine failed to stir her appetite. She only played with the potatoes and eggs. It had been three days since she had eaten at home, and like every true Son of Tong she longed for her bowl of rice.

A few steps away from her a little robin stood diffidently, his head bobbing from side to side. She took a piece of toast and crumbled it on the ground for the robin to eat. Cautiously he pecked at the crumbs until he was confident that Lin would not snatch him. Then he ate with a steady rhythm and Lin watched him, wishing she had pencil and pad to sketch him. The robin finished and was about to take flight.

Lin called to him, "Wait," as softly as possible so that the strains of her voice would not penetrate the bird's delicate body. He stopped and looked at her, his eyes like those of an inquisitive child. She said, "I have fed you, now fly to Scott and tell him I want him to come soon." As if he understood, he nodded his head and flew away swiftly and proudly.

When, later, Scott telephoned to say he was driving over, she asked him, "Who told you I waited and waited for you to call?"

She could almost see a smile breaking out on his face as he said, "A little robin!"

She smiled, for even he would not believe it if she told him. She said, "The cottage is difficult to find. Don't get lost!"

She straightened up the rooms, putting magazines and books together, sweeping up the dust and cigarette ashes. Then she went shopping for groceries, came back, bathed and changed to an apricot-yellow silk cheongsam. It was still warm daylight but she started a fire in the living room. Soon she heard footsteps on the gravel. It was Scott.

"You look like a water color on silk," he said. She took his arm and together they went inside.

An hour later Val came home. From a distance, Val looked as if she towered above Scott, but close up he stood half a head taller than she. Scott took the hand Val extended. She said, "So you're Scott." Lin walked up to them. She said, "You'll like him, Val—you will." She thought of the boy Val was in love with: Terence, a small Irish-Italian who was now in the Navy. Terence liked to work with pastels and one night Val had confided to Lin: "I think I love him because he reminds me of my first stepfather; he took a dickens of a lot from my mother who is as big as I am, and he was so small. I used to feel so awfully sorry for him."

For dinner they had rice that was burned, bean sprouts fried with hamburger meat, and tiny deep-fried shrimps that would have looked like large golden butterflies had Fay cooked them. But their gaiety at table made the unpalatable dinner pleasant.

After tea and coffee Val excused herself and went to visit in the house next door so that Lin and Scott could have the cottage to themselves. They went out on the small veranda. It was not yet dark, though the sun had set. The gentle quietness was agreeably broken by the soft rustle of the leaves and the chirping of insects; the atmosphere and scene was like an old painting by a Chinese master come to life before their eyes. They stayed on the veranda until it became chilly. Then they went back inside.

She sat on the floor in front of the fireplace, her back against the couch; Scott lay on the floor with his head on her lap. He turned his head and his cheek touched her dress. Slowly he moved his face back and forth, for he had grown to love the feel of fine silk. She placed a finger upon his fair hair, feeling how soft it was. She thought: he is as fair as I am dark.

He asked, "What are you going to do?"

She said, "I miss my family, and the studio, and I can't impose on Val forever. I think I'll go home soon. We've all had time to think; tempers may have cooled at home. Perhaps now my family will give us a chance."

The question was in his eyes though not on his lips. She reached down and brushed her mouth on his. She said, "If they haven't changed, I'll leave them."

She had stayed a week at Val's by the time she took the train home. She had intended to stay longer, but Scott's birthday was coming up in a few days. She had looked everywhere for a suitable birthday gift and found nothing that could express her feelings for him. Then she thought of going to Mr. Liu, the dealer in new jade pieces, in his little shop on Grant Avenue.

She was in San Francisco again, going first to the studio. She went over to the porcelains and put her hands on a fine blue-and-white Ming vase. Uncle Fook's face showed he was happy she was back. To him, her week's absence from the ivories and jades had been interminable. He could not bring himself to tell her that she was wrong to have caused the family so much unhappiness. He only said, "Lin, run upstairs and change and hurry down."

She went upstairs and went directly to her room. She changed into peony-pink silk. Fay came in. Lin greeted her. Fay stood by the door and in reply to her greeting said: "You are back."

"Yes, I'm going down to the studio now."

"Lin, are you going to continue to see this Westerner?"

"Yes."

Fay's hands folded together. She said: "Reason has failed. I won't say anymore for you are deaf to my words. But I'm confident you'll come to learn the truth yourself. I only hope the lesson will not be too painful."

"JADE IS HEAVEN," RECORDS THE BOOK OF CHANGES.

"Benevolence lies in its gleaming surface, knowledge in its luminous quality," one reads in the Book of Rites.

Lin was in Mr. Liu's small shop on Grant Avenue, nestled between a pungent-smelling poultry shop and a shop crowded with tubs of snails and bamboo shoots. Mr. Liu was busy with a woman customer, both loudly extolling the beauty of a jade heart the woman had just selected for her future daughter-in-law. Lin was looking over a tray of jade pendants. She loved the feel of jade, cool as the morning dew and smooth as a baby's skin. Mr. Liu was now saying goodbye to his customer and the small shop seemed to rumble with the loud joking between him and the woman. "Perhaps next year this time you will return for a gold bracelet for a grandson," said Mr. Liu. The woman left, chuckling loudly.

"Mr. Liu, I'm having so much difficulty selecting one of these pendants. Every one of them is so lovely, the tiger, the fish, the phoenix, the dragon. . . ."

"Ah, Miss Kwong, for whom are you purchasing jade? for your father . . . uncle. . . ."

She shook her head.

Mr. Liu smiled broadly. "Ah—for a gentleman friend, perhaps."

"Yes," her eyes on the pendants.

"Then we must select accordingly. Give your friend a jade tiger to tell him you think he is courageous; or a horse, who stands for wisdom, dignity and speed. Or perhaps, Miss Kwong, a tortoise, to wish him long life."

She shook her head in disagreement. "No, no, none of these is what I want."

Suddenly the jade fish became clear to her as the carp. How appropriate for Scott, she thought. "Mr. Liu, I want the jade carp. It's for a friend who's a student at Stanford University."

"Ah, Miss Kwong, as the carp is the symbol of ambition, strength and perseverance, as it constantly struggles upstream against the current, so will your university student friend have the strength and perseverance to overcome all obstacles in his studies."

"Mr. Liu, what is the price."

"Miss Kwong, I have known your father and uncle for many years. For you, I will give a large discount."

Mr. Liu was giving her much face by so doing and she thanked him for his generosity. She left the shop, inviting him to visit the family when he had time.

Scott, Lin and Val celebrated Scott's birthday in a small Italian restaurant. After dinner, Val left them. Scott and Lin drove along the beach and parked within sight and sound of the ocean. Lin gave him the jade carp. It hung on a thin cord of red silk and Scott looped it through his belt. That same evening they talked of marriage.

Toward the end of the summer Scott received his orders to report for induction into the army. They decided that in the few weeks remaining before separation they would be married and spend them together. His mother was away in Southern California and so was his grandmother; he would phone his mother to come home to meet Lin as her future daughter-in-law.

On a Sunday noon, Scott and Lin drove over to Berkeley to see Val. The cottage was in more than usual disorder: clothes, shoes and hats were strewn everywhere. Val was in blue jeans and a soiled white shirt, her fair skin shining from lack of makeup. "Everything is a mess," she said, "I'm going to San Diego to meet Terence. I'm so glad to see you two, now please give me a hand."

Lin went to the couch where Val had tossed her cotten dresses and began to fold them. She said, folding a black-and-white check dress as she talked, "Val, Scott and I are getting married. I want you to be my maid of honor."

"Darling, how marvelous! When do you plan to do it?" Val asked, a large hand wiping off the oil on her shiny face as she talked.

"We're getting the license tomorrow."

Val was holding a fluffy pink negligee. She asked, "You have your family's blessing?"

"I'm going to tell them tonight." Val's sigh was very audible. Then quite suddenly she said, dropping the pink negligee: "I will have to phone or wire Terence. He's expecting me tomorrow night. I was to take the bus tomorrow morning."

Lin said, "Val, you haven't seen Terence for months."

Val put a hand to her forehead and made a face. "Darling, to tell you two the truth, I'm torn between wanting to see Terence and staying for the wedding."

Lin went over to her. "Val, don't change your plans. Go and meet Terence. We'll celebrate when you get back." Val put her arms around Lin. She said, "Lin, the most important day of your life and I have to miss it."

"I understand, Val. How long is Terence going to be in San Diego?"

"Nothing's definite but he thinks he'll be two weeks ashore and be shipped out again. Oh Lin, let's not do any more of this. Let's have some coffee."

They went into the kitchen. Val asked, "Where do you two plan to go on your honeymoon?" At this Scott and Lin looked at each other and smiled, for the matter had never even been considered between them. Their expressions gave them away. Val said: "Use my place. I'll be gone for two weeks or more." Before either Lin or Scott had a chance to say anything Val leaped up from her chair, saying she had an extra set of keys in the bedroom.

Lin asked Scott: "Would you like to stay here for our honeymoon?" He held her hands and said that as long as they were together, anywhere would be fine. Lin said, "I would love it here with you. Val is a dear to offer it to us."

Scott and Lin were going down to City Hall to get a marriage license. It was a happy day for Lin, mingled with moments of anxiety, for sometime during the middle of the night she had made up her mind that she would not tell Sun or Fay of her plans until the marriage license was securely in her hands.

She had gone to the studio, dressed in a lavender silk cheongsam. In an hour's time Scott was meeting her to take her to his home to meet his mother. As she closed the front door she suddenly decided that she wanted to tell Fook about her plans. But his greeting was hurried and cross, a rare departure from his usual cheerful self. She was concerned about his attitude and also anxious to confide in him, and in her haste to reach him she accidentally knocked an ashtray to the floor. Fook scolded her loudly and she kept silent until she was sure his anger was out of all proportion to what had happened. Then she asked him, "Second Uncle, what is the matter?" He closed his eyes for a few seconds, then apologized.

"Ah, this morning Mrs. Farrell was here with a porcelain vase she wanted me to look at. She said she had bought it in China years ago. True, it was a beautiful vase, but upon closer examination I detected something was not right. Again and again I looked. The colors and the decorations were excellent. Yes, I told her, it is a Kang Hsi porcelain. Yet somehow I felt something was wrong with it. Then I took a coin and I tapped the vase here and there and then I knew exactly why I had been uneasy. I said to Mrs. Farrell: 'Do you hear the difference in the ring as I tap the coin; original porcelain here and composition there.' She refused to believe me and left in great anger. She has upset me, and like a fool, I looked at the vase for no fee. Now tell me, don't you think white people are absolutely abominable? Are they not without shame, these white devil-women? How they take advantage of us Sons of Tong. . . ."

On and on Fook ranted. Always, when Lin heard these unfair accusations, this blanket indictment of a whole people for the misdeed of one, she shuddered, and she shuddered all the more when she remembered it was the first time she had ever heard her beloved uncle talk so. The desire to confide in him left her and she walked out of the studio and waited in the street for Scott.

THE FIRST THING LIN NOTICED AS SHE STEPPED INTO THE home of Mrs. Hayes was the wallpaper in the foyer. It was a lovely medallion design in pale yellow. She wondered if Mrs. Hayes knew that the ancient Chinese had invented wallpaper and that it was not until the fourteenth century that wallpaper was introduced into Europe. Scott and Lin went into the living room and Scott excused himself to call his mother. Lin reached for his hands and held them for a second so that she could feel in them the strength that she needed so much. And Scott, always seeming to know her so well, gave her a smile that reassured her that everything would be all right. She was nervous and her eyes darted aimlessly around the large living room. She saw a porcelain vase on the mantelpiece. Almost automatically she went to it and placed both hands on it. She could tell by the painting of the dragon and the phoenix that it was a Japanese piece probably sold as a Chinese antique.

[201]

"Lin, this is my mother," she heard suddenly. She turned round and saw Mrs. Hayes.

They sat by the unlit fireplace and tea was served. Mrs. Hayes asked about the House of Tong. She pointed to the Japanese vase and said she had had that beautiful Chinese piece for many years. Ah, you have been cheated, Lin thought to herself. They continued to talk, now about Mrs. Marshall, and her blue-and-white porcelains. Then Mrs. Hayes asked Scott if he would look at the vacuum cleaner that Carlotta, the cleaning woman, had been having trouble with all morning. He might as well take his time, said Mrs. Hayes: she wanted to talk to Lin in private for a while.

Once Scott was out of the room, Mrs. Hayes got up from the sofa and went to the bay window. Suddenly Lin felt an ominous note in the air. Mrs. Hayes turned from the window to face her. Her handsome face was unsmiling. Lin clutched the arm of her chair. Mrs. Hayes said: "Miss Kwong, I will come straight to the point. I do not wish you to marry my son." Words continued to flow from her mouth. Lin hardly heard what she said, for after the shock came a hot feeling of hurt pride. She caught her reflection in a mirrored wall and was fiercely proud that her head was held high, but every ounce of effort in her was used to hold back the tears.

Scott came back to the living room and at once he felt the tension; his face assumed an anxious look. He went over to Lin and asked, "Is anything wrong?"

She said, "Your mother and I have been talking about us. She doesn't wish us to marry."

He looked at her in disbelief. Lin rose from the chair and said, "Scott, take me home now, please!"

He said, "No, Lin, not just yet." He walked over to where Mrs. Hayes stood and faced her. He said in quiet anger: "You have done a terrible thing. I never thought this could come from you. Lin and I are getting married."

Mrs. Hayes held on tightly to a wing chair. She spoke, her voice louder with each succeeding statement: "How can you do this to me? How can you hope to establish yourself with such a marriage? How can you expect to keep your friends if you marry this way? My own friends—what will they say?"

Lin could listen to no more. She snatched her purse and coat and ran out of the house. Scott ran after her and caught up with her. He put his arms around her. "Take me home," she said. They got into the car. Alone together now, she put her head on his shoulder and cried hot, bitter tears.

He said, "I would give anything to relive this day so that this might not have happened; never, never, I will never let you be hurt like this again." He started the car. "We're going down to City Hall to get a marriage license."

She said, "No . . . no . . . let's wait. . . ."

He turned to face her. He said, "Were my mother's words so true that they could separate us."

She said, "No." Then took his hand and said, "Let's go down to City Hall."

At the civic square, Scott parked the car. As he opened the car door for her, the bitter tears had stopped. Lin smiled up at him as she pulled out a compact to powder her face. Arm in arm they went to the office of the marriage license clerk. One other couple was there, and then it was their turn.

The young clerk asked politely what it was they wanted.

Scott and Lin looked at each other and smiled. Scott said, "Just what everyone else here wants . . . we want a marriage license."

The clerk did not smile. Lin suspected nothing, yet a sense of fear obsessed her. It increased when the clerk excused himself saying he would be back. She reached for Scott's hand. The clerk came back with another man whom he introduced as Mr. Riley. Mr. Riley asked Scott and Lin to step into his office. Every instinct within her told Lin that something was wrong and she wanted to flee, but Scott held on to her and led her gently inside.

They sat next to each other, Mr. Riley standing before his desk facing them. His hands were raised palms upward in a gesture of helplessness. He said, "I'm deeply sorry about all this." He reached for a black book on his desk. He opened it to where a bookmark showed. He sighed, then looked at Scott and Lin again to say: "Let me tell you how indignant I am myself about this. Certainly there will come a day when such unfairness will end, but as things stand now, this is the law."

He sat down on his swivel chair and put on a pair of glasses. He read from the black book, his voice a soft monotone: "In the State of California the Civil Code provides that all marriages of white persons with Negroes, Mongolians, members of the Malay race, or mulattoes are illegal and void. It also provides that no license may be issued authorizing any such marriages."

Mr. Riley put the book down and took his glasses off. He rose from his chair and walked to the window. He stared out at the street, talking, talking, telling them that whenever he had to explain the law in similar situations it was heartbreaking to him. He turned away from the window and to his relief he found that Lin and Scott had already left his office.

They were in the car. Scott said: "Let's drive up to Nevada now! I'm sure we can get married up there!"

The outward poise that Lin had shown was only the silence of one stunned, and the clutching to a desperate assurance that the injustice was not against herself but against an abstract entity. Now her assurance fell apart, and racking cries of hurt and humiliation burst from within her. She cowered against the door of the car: it was the way she felt—she was nothing. "Take me home!" she cried.

A silence followed. She was alone in the world; even Scott had become a stranger to her. She heard him say "I love you," his voice trembling, in his eyes the hurt that she should sever herself from him.

Then reason returned and she was in his arms, but the tears would not stop. His firm hold on her told her that she did matter after all. Tighter . . . tighter . . . her fingers pressed on his back to tell him to hold her tighter.

"Let's go over to Berkeley!" he said.

"Hurry! Hurry!"

Too young for bitterness, too good for bitterness, their faces were happy as they approached the bridge.

Now they stood in front of the house that was built to look like a Swiss chalet, and as she looked up she said, "Darling, the place is ours for a whole week!" Then hand in hand together they ran up the terrazzo steps.

THEY WALKED TOGETHER UNTIL ONLY A SINGLE STREAK of dusky pink remained. Now the skies were dark and they returned to the tiny cottage. Inside it was warm; a fire had been burning, though now only the ashes remained. He busied himself with kindling wood and she poured tea from the pot that had been kept close to the fireplace.

Now the flames burned high again. They sat on the floor, their backs against the couch. The tea was cool and they drank from thick glass tumblers.

"Come closer," he said.

She moved closer to him and her face was against the soft flesh of his throat. She brushed her mouth against him, over and over again. She pulled away slightly so that she could see his face. In the dark, lit only by the flare of the fire, his hair was a pale yellow. Now she knew the rest of him, that his waist was firm and that it blended in a straight line to his narrow hips. She took hold of his hands and held them to her face and knew that in moments of love, they were hot and moist. "Say you love me," she said, and he answered and she thought of his voice in those moments of love when not words but cries of bitter-sweetness mingled with hers.

He said: "I'll always think of you whenever I see wild lilacs." He had bought her the sweet essence, a red cotton dress and a pair of straw sandals.

He moved so that his face was now against the area that was soft behind her ear. She reached to touch his hair, soft and silklike, touching and seeing it in a way to remember the moment so that in looking back she would not need to say that it could have been a greater moment; she would let nothing be trivial, allow nothing to be prosaic.

He said: "You have such beautiful hair."

She felt elation, but she protested: "I have the hair of the southern Chinese; it is thick and slightly coarse. Your hair is silk, mine is but humble cotton."

He shook his head and murmured, "No . . . no . . . no. . . ."

She saw that the fire had burned low. Together they threw fresh wood on it. The flames flared up yellow and gold, like a wild abstract painting. The sudden snapping noise of the burning wood made her dart backward. Shadows of furniture on the wall, magnified and distorted, moved up and down with the action of the flame; a lemon in a print suddenly shone out in the dark.

She lay on the floor. He put a pillow under her head. She raised her hands, the fingers spread and arched. He bent down to kiss her.

"What day is it today?" she asked.

"Does it matter?" he asked, his face against hers.

"How many days have we been here?"

"Four . . . five . . . six . . . I don't know. . . ."

Tomorrow they would look at the morning paper for

the date to see how close it was to the day he had to report
to the induction center.

"Come closer to me on the floor. . . ."

Now they were both on the floor. With his hand on her
slender waist he pulled her to him so that they both rested
sideways. Their bodies were pressed together.

"Darling, let's go into the bedroom . . ." he said.

"Yes . . . much better inside . . ." she recalled their
experience two evenings before.

It was a bright evening and the full moon outside shone
generously enough into this room that was even smaller
than the living room. He unbuttoned his shirt, took it off,
and tossed it in a corner. Her red cotton dress buttoned
in the back; she called to him for help. He went to her,
and one by one undid the buttons that started under the
neck and reached below the waist. She kicked off her straw
sandals and stepped out of her dress. It dropped to the
floor and her naked feet felt the cool cotton. Now her
naked feet felt the soft silk of her lingerie.

Now all she wore was the essence of lilac. He stepped
back to look at her, then reached out for her and held her
tightly. His trembling hands searched out the hairpins in
her chignon. She shook her head lightly and her straight
hair fell below her shoulders. She stood on her tiptoes,
her arms tightly around him. The words, brushed upon
silk, of a poet of long ago came again to her. She quoted
aloud in translation, for he too liked the words.

"Tears and sorrows, constant as the moon,
  Happiness the rainbow seen in a lifetime,
  Why wait 'til an aftertime when the wine cup is in the hand,
  Why wait 'til an aftertime when the coin jingles in the
      purse."

Now she told him to hurry as she sought the warmth of the cover until he could join her. With no benefit of moonlight she saw his silhouette as he undressed. He tossed his slacks to the floor; they fell where the moon shone and in the brightness she saw the gleaming eyes of the tiny jade carp.

He went to her. His mouth was on hers. His hands were trembling; frantically she reached for one of them and placed it on her breast.

SCOTT WAS TAKING HIS BASIC TRAINING IN CAMP ROBERTS, California. He was to be there for several months. One October Saturday afternoon, in the uniform of an army private that at first made him a stranger to her, Scott met Lin at the studio. From then on he came out to see her every weekend. But the brief hours were frustrating, for they remembered their days in Berkeley and now they were never alone. In the studio, Fook was always there, good and sympathetic, forever unsuspecting, never realizing Scott and Lin wanted privacy.

The autumn days continued warm. As Lin's hands touched the rim of a blue-and-white vase, she wondered if the September days in Berkeley had really existed. Then the weather turned chilly; the night biting cold; the autumn season was ending. She put away her silks and wore fur-lined woolen dresses, the collars buttoned high on the neck, the sleeves long and snug, the slits not quite as high as the ones she wore before.

Then winter was here and Scott was home on a thirty-day furlough upon completion of his basic training. He had instructions to report to Camp Kilmer, New Jersey, after the furlough; Camp Kilmer was Embarkation Camp for overseas duty.

The day before, the January breeze had been almost warm, and it had rained. Now the air was biting cold, a good sign. It meant that the evening would stay dry, and the Chinese could celebrate the last day of the Year of the Horse both indoors and outdoors.

"Scott, you take care of Lin!" Val's voice rang out as she made a dash for the train to return to Berkeley.

"I will!" cried Scott.

"He will!" echoed Lin.

Val found a seat on the train. She opened the window and called out again: "Lin, Scott, thanks again for that wonderful dinner!"

"We'll do it again soon!"

The train started. Val waved. "Say Happy New Year to your family and give my best to your brother when you write him!"

Lin's fur-lined violet-blue cheongsam did not keep her warm; the chill entered through the slits of the skirt. With both hands she held on to Scott who wore his overcoat with the collar turned up. He took her hand and slipped it into a pocket, holding it there with his. Her other hand remained on his arm. They left the Ferry Building and crossed over to the financial district.

There was no cable car in sight. They would walk the distance back to watch the celebration to end the old year.

"It's good to see you in civilian clothes again," she said.

Almost a week of Scott's furlough had already been

spent. Lin had promised to write to the State of Nevada to inquire if they could be married there. She had promised him she would write before he began his furlough. But she had not done so. In the lonely hours of the night when another self woke her from sleep she knew why. She dreaded the possibility of hurt and humiliation again. She had wept, but not for long, and fallen back to sleep vowing to herself that she would write the next day. The next day the letter to Nevada had again been put off: Fay had wanted to go shopping with her in preparation for the New Year—food, fruit, tea, red paper, joss sticks—it was an annual ritual with Fay; Fook had gone to an auction; Sun had needed her help in the store: a clerk had been ill and the Tai Ming Company was busy with customers buying porcelains for the New Year; Val had come over to see her . . . she had found many reasons for putting off the letter she dreaded to write.

In the excitement of Scott's first day of furlough he had forgotten to ask her what the answer was from Nevada; then Fook had celebrated with them for a whole day; Scott's grandmother had visited him; tonight it was the Chinese New Year's Eve and they had invited Val to dine out with them; the days had slipped by and the letter was still unsent.

Now there were only two more steep hills to climb before they reached the area of festivities. An occasional firecracker sounded. The tall streetlamp with the golden dragon entwined about it was in sight; the paper lanterns knocked against each other. She shivered; the wind penetrated her thin stockings. He put an arm around her shoulder to warm her.

An idea occurred to her. "Scott, we needn't bother to

phone to Nevada. Why don't we just go there? If we can, fine; if we can't, we'll travel on."

He pressed her hand tightly to let her know he agreed.

"We can go on to Utah," she said, "or is Washington closer?"

"We'll worry about it then."

"You don't know?"

"No."

"I never liked geography either."

A single, steep hill remained to be climbed. They stopped. Her face was radiant; the brisk wind was kind to her skin.

"You look lovely," he said.

"Thank you."

He asked, "Are you going to tell your family?"

"Yes—they'll be unhappy but they'll accept it later. I know them."

They started the climb up the hill, the Catholic Church was directly ahead of them.

"Scott, are you going to tell your mother?"

"Yes, I'm going to tell her."

Halfway up the hill she felt tired. They stood against a doorway.

"Let's leave tomorrow," Scott said.

"Give me a few days. I'd like to buy a few things. I'd like a very sheer dressing gown—maybe two—a white one and a black one and slippers to match."

"Lin, don't bother. . . . I'd rather you wear nothing but your lilac."

She laughed.

Grant Avenue was crowded. They went to see the sidewalk flower stands put up especially for the New Year.

The azaleas, camellias, peonies and chrysanthemums were beautiful. She bent over a bowl of lily narcissus bulbs to smell the loveliest fragrance in all flowers. Friends greeted her, young and old, and she introduced Scott to them but conversations were impossible in the crowded, noisy street.

She heard the unmistakable sound of mah-jongg games. She stood on tiptoes to reach Scott's ear to confide: "My uncle will be playing mah-jongg until daylight. He does it every New Year's Eve. Let's go to the studio."

It was the first time they had really been alone. Without turning on the lights she led him into Fook's little office. There she turned on the lamp. He kissed her, and she led him to a small couch. He kissed her again.

"Scott! Scott! Do you ever think of our days in Berkeley?"

"Darling, every minute!"

His mouth was on her throat.

"Scott! Scott! I can't believe we're alone. This is the first chance we've had!"

"Lin, I love you . . . I love you. . . ."

"Scott! Scott!"

"Darling, your lilac . . . how I love your lilac. . . ."

"Scott, undo my dress. . . ."

His trembling hands fumbled with her silk frog buttons. The neckline was undone; his hands moved across her breast. Suddenly a rattle sounded from the front door. They jumped up, startled. The rattling persisted. She buttoned her dress and went to open the door. A huge bunch of golden chrysanthemums greeted her. Behind the flowers emerged Mr. Chew, a flower grower and close friend of the family.

"Mr. Chew."

"Bo Lin, Bo Lin, I have some flowers for your family."

She would have to invite him in.

"So good of you, so good of you. Come inside."

"There is no one in the home."

"No, Mother and Father are at the theater. They will not be home until well after midnight and possibly later if they dine afterward. Second Uncle is playing mah-jongg."

"Bo Lin, you know I bring flowers to your family every New Year." He handed them to her.

"I know. You are always so kind to remember us. The chrysanthemums are exceptionally beautiful this year."

Such generosity would necessitate consideration on her part. "Mr. Chew, you must stay and have a cup of tea."

Tonight there would be no gracious request that the hostess need not bother about tea, for it was New Year's Eve and all formalities would be observed. Mr. Chew sat down to await his tea.

"I was about to leave when I glanced through the window and saw evidence of some light in here."

Scott came out; he was presented to Mr. Chew.

Mr. Chew knew little English and said, "How do?"

Lin offered Mr. Chew a cup of tea and a plate of almond cookies. She signaled to Scott: just a tiny cup of tea; he would be on his way in no time.

Mr. Chew put the cup to his mouth.

"Ah! It is too hot! I must let it cool!"

He stared at Scott, looking at him with candid eyes.

"Bo Lin, this Westerner is very pale; is he in good health?"

"Yes, that is his natural coloring."

"Bo Lin, this Westerner is quite thin, though quite tall. Is he a strong man?" continued the weather-beaten flower grower.

"Yes, he is a strong man; he is not a bulky person, that is all."

"Bo Lin, have I seen him before? Is he perhaps a clerk in some shop downtown where I take my flowers?"

"No, he is not a clerk anywhere."

"Ah, it is only my imagination. It is difficult for me; I cannot tell one white face from another!"

"Mr. Chew, your tea should be right for drinking now!"

"Ah! My tea!" He finished his tea. "Bo Lin, save the cookies for yourself. I do not eat sweets."

Lin smiled—he would soon be on his way. But the weather-beaten face turned to Scott again and turned back to face Lin. In a voice with overtones of paternalism he asked: "Bo Lin, this Westerner is merely a good friend?"

"Yes, he is a good friend."

"Nothing more than a good friend?"

"A good friend."

Mr. Chew's tanned finger was in the air as he said: "Merely good friends . . . that is all right . . . remember, we are Sons of Tong."

Mr. Chew's eyes lit up with enthusiasm. "Ah, Bo Lin, has Hubert been to see you?" Hubert was his son, a student of business administration at the University of California, a friend of Kiang's.

"We have conversed over the phone."

"He will be graduating in June. He will join me in my flower business."

According to Hubert, Mr. Chew, his father would join *him*. Hubert's plans for expansion had often been expounded. He would pack asters and chrysanthemums in dry ice and ship them all over the Eastern seaboard.

Hubert would, as he had often told Lin and Kiang, make
money "hand over fist." Kiang and Hubert were good
friends but their common theme, "anything you can do, I
can do better," caused occasional friction.

"Bo Lin, you must come see our new house! I will ask
Hubert to drive you over."

Mr. Chew had recently bought a beautiful house in his
son's name adjacent to their large flower farm in the
suburbs. Money accumulated through years of hard work
and old-world frugality had been spent at Hubert's insistence. "We've got to show the old folks how to live.
What do they do with all their money? Put it in the bank
for a measly $3\frac{1}{2}$ percent interest!" Hubert had forgotten
that the old folks were sending him and his brothers and
sisters to college.

"You are very kind. I would like to see your new home.
Mother, Father and Second Uncle would like to see it too.
We will all go together."

"Bo Lin, from the large window in our living room
you can see acres and acres of flowers. It is a magnificent
view."

Mr. Chew loved the things he grew; to Hubert, they
represented dollars and cents.

And if this were not enough, all of Hubert's upper
teeth protruded.

"Bo Lin, you would like living in a house such as
ours." His opened mouth grew wider than before.

"Bo Lin, you are such a pretty girl." His eyes became
wistful. "My Hubert is a good boy."

"Hubert is a smart young man."

Mr. Chew got up from his chair. Goodbyes were said.
He headed for the door. Scott and Lin signaled their relief

to each other with their eyes. Mr. Chew stopped and turned around. He said, "Bo Lin! Bo Lin! I have forgotten something!"

"What?" Her voice was almost sharp.

He reached into a pocket and took out a red envelope with a coin in it, a gift for the New Year.

"Mr. Chew! I am a grown girl now. It is not necessary!"

"Yes, accept it; you may until you marry and then you must give."

"Thank you, Mr. Chew. A Happy New Year to you."

"A Happy New Year to you and your family. Peace of heart and prosperity to all."

Mr. Chew was gone. Lin switched off the overhead light.

"I thought he'd never leave!"

"Lin!" She was in his arms. He kissed her. "Let's go back inside."

"Yes, and we'll turn the light off in there."

With his arm on her slender waist they returned to the little room. The mood they were in earlier had gone and would not return. Mr. Chew was still with them. Together they laughed aloud until the spirit of the inquisitive flower grower left them.

She lay on the sofa and kicked off her high heels. She reached for him and held him.

"Where were we before?"

"We'll start all over again."

"A fine idea."

He kissed her and it was as if they had never been interrupted. His mouth was on her throat, . . . then the tips of her ears. "Scott, my dress."

Again his hands worked on the silk buttons, so difficult

to undo. Slowly, slowly, one by one. She would not help him, for she wanted the feel of his hands as they went from neckline to bodice, to waistline, to skirt, down to the slit. More kisses before he undid the straps of her lingerie.

"My God! What was that?" Scott jumped up, terrified. She too sat up.

"Firecrackers . . . it must be midnight . . . the Year of the Goat," she said, an air of resignation in her voice.

Scott turned on the light. He was shaken. The sounds of explosion continued. She said, "You should see it . . . strings of giant firecrackers hung from the roof to the street in every building; smoke and the smell of sulfur everywhere."

Her laughter was mingled with tears. "Scott, it was so funny . . . you look so funny too. . . ."

Scott came out of his trance. He turned the light off again. Part of his attention was still on the firecrackers as he bent over her to say: "Like a battlefield."

Softly she answered, "Yes, war must sound like that. . . ." She herself would undo the straps of her underthings.

Voices sounded outside the little room. Hurriedly they sat up. With deft hands she buttoned herself and smoothed her hair as Scott tightened his belt and straightened his tie.

It was Fook and seven friends replete with herb brandy, food, chairs, mah-jongg sets, and two mah-jongg tabletops. Jovially Fook greeted Scott and Lin.

"The fuse blew out where we were playing. We played by candlelight until it became impossible!"

Lin asked, "Couldn't you have used more candles?"

"Aha! Everyone except myself was cheating."

In the same vein she asked, "Couldn't one of you have changed the fuse?"

"Everyone was either too drunk or too stupid!"

Scott and Lin declined the invitation to join the party to eat barbecued pork, fried noodles and won ton.

They left the studio. The cold wind hit them. He took her hand and slipped it in with his into the pocket of his overcoat. She put her head on his shoulder. Softly she began to cry and both knew that this time the tears were genuine.

"MY ADVICE HAS BEEN BITTER BUT GOOD, DISPLEASING but loyal, still you do not listen. I can do nothing more. But of this I am certain, Lin. In time, for you and this Westerner, one will head East, the other West, making you two so far apart that when together you will be but two strange visitors in a strange land." So spoke Sun, his voice low and soft, his lean face unhappy and stern. Lin had told him she and Scott were leaving for Nevada to get married.

He turned around and faced the photograph of Grandfather Kwong and the family. He shook his head and sighed, as if apologizing to his father that he had been so unsuccessful with his children. He turned around again and asked, "Have you told your mother?"

"Not yet."

This would cause Fay the deepest pain, he knew; in bed she tossed in restless sleep and he himself could not sleep knowing she was unhappy. He knew how unsuccessful he had been with his children; he did not impute to her this lack of success. Fate was against Fay and fate had been cruel since the first time illness had prevented her sailing to the House that Tai Ming Built. He felt sudden anger at Lin, unspoken words choking in his throat, urging him to say that he washed his hands of an ungrateful daughter, and that she should run off immediately and spare Fay any further unhappiness. But he was a man deliberate in his speech so that he only dismissed her with one final vigorous wave of his hand and turned back to his abacus and account books.

Lin left the office and headed for the house to tell Fay. She found her mother reading the newspaper in her bedroom, sitting in a rattan chair by the window with her back to the sun. "The war news is bad," she said as she saw Lin. She put the paper down. She lowered her head so that the sun could shine directly on her neck, which ached, because of her sleepless nights. "Was there a letter from Kiang today?" she asked.

"No," Lin answered.

"Ah! No letter still! Delivery service from overseas is quite hopeless!"

Her neck felt too warm now. She rested her head against the chair so that the sun shone on her face. She closed her eyes: Kiang had been granted several days at home before overseas duty; since shipping out there had only been one brief letter from him. The news about the war in the Pacific was bad; her whole body shook suddenly. She sat up. Her eyes still closed, she turned to a fragrance of lilacs. Her daughter had come to talk, she could tell. Her hands tightened on the arms of the chair; this too would be unpleasant. "You have something to tell me?" she asked.

"Scott and I are going to Nevada tomorrow to get married."

Fay said nothing, for she knew words would be futile; her daughter talked and looked as one in complete command of herself; let her discover for herself in experience and maturity that one can never be certain what fate would decree; had she ever dreamed that the little girl with the fringe of hair across her forehead would someday tell her a thing like this?

Fay's silence was disconcerting. Lin said, "I'm going down to the studio now."

Fay raised a hand to beckon her to remain. "A second . . . a second," she said. She rose from her chair and slowly walked over to a chest of drawers. From a jewelry box she selected a pair of gold bracelets and a jade heart on a gold chain and wrapped them in red paper. "Wear these on your wedding day," she said and walked away from Lin to return to her chair in the sun.

Lin went to the studio; she was grateful that no visitors were there. From Fook she would hear words of assurance that what she was doing was right; she was certain of that.

She found him in his small office, his round head bent low over a vase he held lovingly in his small hands. It was a piece she had never seen before; white, thin, the glaze crackled and the form severely simple.

She asked, "Is this a piece you have just bought?"

"Not exactly, but is it not lovely! Of the Sung period; originally made for the Imperial household."

He looked up at her, the small vase clutched tightly for safety against his chest. Nothing must happen to this valuable piece that would stand among the other favorite Sung pieces in his own room, never to be sold. He saw in her face that her affair of the heart weighed on her. He sighed and returned his gaze to the crackled vase. He smiled, looked up at her again and asked, "Would you like to know how I got this piece?"

At the moment she didn't care, but dutifully she said yes, and sat down near him, knowing how long his account could be.

He began: "Last night, my three friends and I had our weekly dinner in a restaurant, and after, as usual, made plans for our mah-jongg game. We could not play at Suen's apartment as we normally do because his wife was ill. I ruled out our home because your mother is also not feeling well. We ruled out the third person's apartment because it has rats! There was only Bing's place to go to. Good, we said. Bing is that fine old man who is a partner in the bookstore, around the corner. We went up to Bing's apartment, a tiny place with no room to walk about when the mah-jongg table and chairs are set up. There in that small room, suddenly, what do I see? What do I see? Among a pile of books and photographs I see this lovely vase. I stopped and stared! I said, could it be! Could it be! I reached for it and examined it and I said, 'Bing, where did you get this exquisite Sung piece?'

"He scratched his head and said that years ago in China a rascal had given it to him in lieu of a debt outstanding, thrusting it in his unwilling hands and shouting in the presence of witnesses that the debt was paid in full with the exchange of the vase. Then the rascal ran off and Bing had never seen him again. But, as Bing tells the story, he grew to love the vase, feeling its shape was in commendable taste. The crackle intrigued him, making him wonder, as he looked at it, what greater rascal than that rascal would take a knife to scratch up the vase. So Bing kept the vase, bringing it with him to America and there in his small room it had stood for years.

"I said to Bing: 'Bing! This is a genuine Sung piece! The scratched effect is deliberate!' He said to me, incredulous, 'Elder Brother Fook, is this truly a Sung piece?'

"I examined it further; yes! I said. I said to Bing, 'Bing! There is no mistake in the consummate skill and material of the artist of the Sung period!'

"He said to me, 'Elder Brother Fook, you admire the piece, you know the piece; I present it to you!'

"Astonished, I said, 'I cannot accept such a valuable thing; it will be depriving you of a thing of beauty.'

"He said to me: 'But I did not even accord it a special place. It was here—among these other old things, see! next to an old pair of stockings. How ashamed I am!'

"I said to him: 'But you love it! You find it beautiful!'

"He said to me: 'Ah, indeed! It got to be a pleasant habit for me to fondle it each night as I passed it to go to the bathroom.'

"I said to him: 'How then can I accept it! I cannot deprive you! It would not be right!'

"He urged me! I refused! He urged me further! I steadfastly refused but the truth was I wanted it dearly, but I could not deprive the dear old man of it. I tried to think how I could have it yet not have my conscience sore. I thought of offering money, but it would have been in poor taste to drag in money."

Fook paused for breath. He looked at Lin. He was only slightly offended that she did not seem at all interested. He continued: "Lin, is it not touching that Bing found the vase beautiful? A fine old man; there is virtually nothing about the history of the Middle Kingdom that he cannot tell you, but he does not know a thing about its fine arts. Yet, Lin, something was given him that he had no wish for; then using his own eyes he found it beautiful and soon his heart and mind told him he loved it. Now, is that not how everyone should judge and decide, whether it be a painting or a sculpture, or a dish of food, and certainly, Lin, a human being. . . ."

Her slim hands were upon his hand; they lay there briefly until she took it and placed it on her cheek. Always she would look at life through art, as he did, discarding the bad and the distasteful, seeking forever with honest eyes, heart and mind the fine and the beautiful.

His eyes were once again on the vase. He said: "Lin, I almost thought this piece was destined for me. Let me explain. Quite a few years ago when I was at the House that Tai Ming Built, I took several days holiday in Shanghai with my children and their mother. It was a hot summer day and we had been traveling throughout the city. We were very tired and hot when we got back to our hotel. The children and their mother took a nap while overhead a large electric fan whirled.

"I started out to see the city again by myself. There is much to see in Shanghai, much that is lovely and hideous, and always a conglomeration of people about the streets all day. Then suddenly I saw in a shop window a small white vase with a crackle glaze which I guessed might be a Sung piece. I hurried in; I looked at it closely from the window; I liked it; I wanted it!

"The clerk came over. I asked him the price. Alas, he spoke only Shanghai dialect, not understanding one bit my Cantonese. We talked, we shouted, we flung our arms about—we got nowhere. I took the vase out and examined it closely, looking at the foot rim, checking to see if there was a seal and so on. I knew it was a Sung piece! I said in

English to myself, 'Beautiful—beautiful.' Why at that moment I said it in English I will never know, perhaps because I get so excited when I come upon a piece unexpectedly.

"The clerk exclaimed, 'Let us converse in English. I studied abroad in England.' In English I asked the price of the vase. He preferred to exchange talk about our educations. Repeatedly he asked where I got my degree. Repeatedly I asked the price of the vase. Then thinking if I told him something he would come back to the vase, I snatched at an answer. I said, 'Stanford University; California; I am an instructor of science there.'

"The fool was impressed! He asked what kind of science. I said 'profound science.' He asked in awe, 'What is that?'

"And Lin, you know my English, I cannot say the 'r' so that it doubly confused him for I really meant to say political science, not profound science! He asked me further, 'Sir, what is that science?' Now I was confused; I could not even remember what kind of professor I had pretended to be. I said, 'It is something new in the West! Nowadays America does not take everything from England as once it did.'

"The fool was even more impressed. I stamped my foot and asked him to talk about the vase. He looked like one in a daydream. I stamped out of the place, my mind made up I would return tomorrow for the piece.

"I could not go to the fool's shop until late the next day. But ah! it had been sold—sold to a Britisher, the fool explaining that an Oxford graduate had come in at the noon hour and bought it.

"So Lin, when I first saw this vase at Bing's place I thought it was my destiny and fate to have it. But now, upon further examination I recall the one in Shanghai was slightly different for on this one the crackle is better defined!"

Lin poured a cup of tea for him. "This is not too hot but I think you should drink it nevertheless."

The tea soothed his tired throat.

Lin asked: "Now then, Second Uncle, you steadfastly refused Uncle Bing's generous offer. How is it you're in possession of it now?"

"Ah! This morning! Early this morning a clerk from Bing's store came here with it. Bing had wrapped it up in a dish towel, wrapped a piece of red paper on the outside, tied it with red string and had instructed his clerk to say that the vase was mine to keep. Such a fine, generous man! Now of course I will keep it and think of something appropriate to give to him."

She had almost forgotten what it was she had come to tell him. Now she remembered and said: "Second Uncle, Scott and I are leaving tomorrow morning for Nevada. We're going to get married."

"Why must you run all the way up there? Can't you get married here in San Francisco? I would like to come to your wedding."

She turned away from him and looked toward the floor. She said, "The California state law doesn't allow such marriages."

Fook's voice, steady and soft, urged, "No, no, Lin—hold your head high—hold your head high—always!"

She raised her head and held it high. She smiled at him. He slapped a hand upon the desk and said, "Lin, indeed you are a beauty! I am so proud of you! Ah—and that fragrance, how delightful it is; I had meant to tell you all this time."

They rose from their seats. Fook paused; he said, "Stupid! How stupid of me! Lin, tomorrow you're getting married; I must give you a wedding present. Now then, what shall I give you? I must think. Run along. Lin, you run along outside and let me think."

She said, "Second Uncle, you needn't spend money on me, truly."

He said, "You run along."

She was standing by the black lacquer screen when he went to her, holding an object loosely wrapped in red silk. He offered it to her; she accepted it with both hands. It was a gold filigree ornament for the hair, studded with paste in imitation of rubies and seed pearls.

Almost in a whisper, she said, "Second Uncle, this is lovely."

He said, "Isn't it? May I suggest that when you wear this on your hair, you do not wear earrings and that your dress should be a simple one of a single shade of color."

She said, "I shall remember that. Scott will love this pin; he will!"

He said, "I've had this for many, many years though you have never seen it. Let me tell you about it.

"Years ago when I was a young university student in Canton, I spent many hours in a teahouse, always a book in my hands, eating and drinking as I read. Foolish one I was, for there is no more noisy place than a teahouse in Canton! Nonetheless, I went there almost daily, always with a book. At that particular time, I was enamored of the beautiful Yang Kuei Fei and every book that had ever been written about her I read avidly.

"So one afternoon, I was reading a book about this famous beauty and, like the exhibitionist I was at that time, I stood the book up high to let others know I was a man interested in classical literature, standing it high to let all see the title and the beautiful drawing of Yang Kuei Fei on the cover. Soon a stranger came up to me, a man much older than I and very well dressed. He said that he too liked classical literature and we talked. I talked my head off for I was young, and that others must be impressed by my mind was then important to me. Suddenly he assumed a most serious face and nudged me to get close to him. He then whispered in my ear that he had something very beautiful, very valuable and very rare, to sell. I asked what. He asked in confidential tones if I could be trusted. I assured him I could be.

"He whispered to me that, hidden in his pocket, was a relic once possessed by Yang Kuei Fei. Amazed, I pressed him to tell me what it was and to let me see it. He whispered to me that it was a beautiful hairpin she had worn on that tragic day when she hanged herself with a silk scarf on the pear tree. He took something out of his pocket and, putting it in the crook of his arm, he gave me a quick look. I was excited beyond words! He gave me the price; it was exorbitant!

"He continued to talk only in whispers, always looking furtively about him as he talked. I said to him that I could not consider buying it if it were stolen property. He banged the table in indignation. I was fearful I had lost the chance to own the relic. I apologized to him and even filled his cup. He whispered to me that his reason for secrecy was this: he was a well known dealer, and many collectors who dealt with him frequented the teahouse where we were sitting. Often he had been able to exact a greater price for a piece by promising that when Yang Kuei Fei's hairpin was to be put on the market the buyer would be warned before anyone else. This was his reason for secrecy, for he had made the promise to too many people.

"The sum was more than I could afford. Fool that I was, I told him that my monthly allowance was rigidly budgeted by your grandmother and asked him for advice. The rascal immediately invented a story for me to tell your grandmother. Shame to say, I followed his advice, hurrying to your grandmother to tell her that it was absolutely necessary that I have such an amount immediately, for fire had destroyed half the buildings on the campus and contributions were being implored from all who could give.

"The hairpin was mine! The rascal said I was the recipient of a treasure many would pay ten times as much for, and that in return for this favor I must keep the purchase a secret for the period of one month; one whole month, he emphasized. I did just that, hiding the hairpin under my blankets and clutching it as I slept. The month was up. I took it to my history professor, for he was a well known collector.

"I told him the story, breathless with excitement. At the end of the story I noticed that his face had grown sympathetic. He shook his head and said, 'Poor, poor Fook.' I asked the reason. He took the hairpin and explained to me how by examining the material and the method of workmanship it could not possibly have been made in the Tong Dynasty; and further, he doubted very much that Yang Kuei Fei ever possessed any rubies and pearls that were not genuine.

"I was shattered! He offered me a cup of tea. He said that what I got was at least a beautiful thing. He waved a white cloth at me, waving and waving while I sat wondering what he was doing, yet not asking. After all, a man had a right to be eccentric in his own home. Finally he said: 'That hairpin will come into use someday; perhaps a sweetheart or a wife will one day wear it. But this—what can I do with *this?*'

" 'What do you mean?' I asked.

"He replied: 'My story to my mother was that I needed the money to pay for two dear friends' funerals. But in my younger days, it was not a hairpin but a precious square of the white silk scarf that Yang Kuei Fei hanged herself with on the pear tree!' "

Lin clapped her hands in spontaneous applause. She said, "For shame, Second Uncle, surely you learned a lesson!"

He said, "For shame, indeed! Thereafter I gave my affection only to women of impeccable character!"

She laughed and shook a finger at him. "You must tell Scott that story someday. He'll enjoy it so."

He said, "Yes . . . the hairpin will look lovely against your black, lacquered hair. But Lin, I have something else to give you."

She asked, "What?"

He said, "Immediately after the war, I'm going to present you and Scott with tickets on a liner to sail to the House that Tai Ming Built."

In a faltering voice she said, "Second Uncle, you're too good to me."

"Lin, there is a condition."

"What?"

"That I too, sail with you and Scott. Lin, wouldn't it be wonderful for me to realize my dreams with you, Scott, and my family—all of us in the city of Peking."

Tears of happiness were in her eyes. Mistaken, he

sought to console her. "Lin, don't cry; don't cry. Ha! A thought to drive away the tears. How do you think Scott will look dressed in a long gown of blue, sitting in the pavilion upon the hill—a cup of tea, a plate of melon seeds, and your grandfather and grandmother beside him?"

The tears rolled down her cheeks as her laughter pealed out. Soon the tears rolled down Fook's plump, round cheeks as he too laughed and laughed, so that by contrast the ancient stone head of the bodhisattva behind them looked more forbidding than ever.

HIGH UP IN THE LARGE LIVING ROOM, LIN AND SCOTT stood by the window to admire the brilliant January weather. It was Sunday and the organ music for the Mass could be heard. Yesterday it had rained. A dreary morning had given way to a bright afternoon.

"Darling, it's a good sign for our wedding day," Lin said. She wore a red silk cheongsam, for red was the color of joy and happiness. The high color was becoming to her and her skin was delicately tinted by the reflection of sunlight on her dress. Scott caught her in his arms and a hand reached up to touch her cheek. His voice was a mixture of laughter and impatience. "Are you ready to leave now?" he asked. He had come to the house for her luggage; his car was parked around the corner. It was a long drive up to Nevada but she had spent more than an hour showing him her new clothes.

"I'm ready," she said. Her face was suddenly serious, and as quickly it was happy again.

At the bottom of the stairway, she made him stop just

as he was about to open the door. "Put the things down. Hold me," she said softly.

He wore a heavy tweed coat. She could not feel the warmth of his body. She placed a hand on his face.

"Darling, what is it?" he asked.

"Maybe we can't get married in Nevada," she said.

"Has that been on your mind?" he asked.

"Yes, I thought about it last night, and this morning."

"Darling, don't be afraid. Leave everything to me," he said.

He opened the door so that there would be light on the dark landing. "I love you," he said.

She smiled. "I love you," she answered.

A crescendo of organ music sounded as they stepped outside. The Mass was over. A priest in a long robe stood by the church door with eyes toward the bright glare of the sky; before the service, the day had been dull. A Western Union messenger shouted out to ask if he had the correct address. Lin said yes and took a telegram. "It must be from Val to wish us luck," she said, as she tore open the envelope. The message was brief: The United States Government sent its regrets that Kiang had been killed in action in the Pacific.

The church bells rang. A crowd of people gathered to take the cable car back to their homes. Churchgoers hurried into the cable car and those who could not get on stepped aside quickly as the motorman clanged the bell and started his overloaded trolley. Three taxicabs were one behind another and a priest escorted a well dressed couple heading for one of them. The cabs blocked the traffic and a man in a black sedan was impatient with his horn. A police motorcycle roared past Lin and Scott. Her head ached.

"Darling, we can't leave . . ." her voice trailed off and then she was unable to think or speak any further.

"Give me your keys," Scott said.

She handed him the keys. "The studio," she said.

They waited until the noise died down. The shades were drawn and it was semidark in the studio. She leaned against the door. Her head throbbed.

"What am I to do?" she finally asked.

"You'll have to tell your family."

"We can't go to Nevada," she said.

"We can leave later, maybe tonight."

"They'll need me," she said. He wiped away her tears. She started to speak but stopped. A woman's voice sounded through the closed door, reading aloud the date of the Han vase on display in the little window. A man's voice responded. Now together, the voices of the strangers talked while Lin and Scott waited for them to go away.

Lin's eyes moved about, searching for an object on which to concentrate. Without lighting, the porcelains and ivories were only outlines; texture and craftsmanship were obscure. On the opposite wall hung a water color. Even in the dark the picture was too crowded, adding to the hurt and confusion in her mind. She closed her eyes. The telegram was in her hand as she reached up to put her arms around Scott. The message caught her eyes; she dropped it to the floor. Suddenly fingers hard as bronze seemed to dig inside her head: did it mean anything that the news of Kiang's death had arrived just as she was leaving to be married?

The strangers outside were gone. Scott asked, "If you don't feel you should leave tonight, will you go with me tomorrow?"

"Scott, don't ask anything of me now," she said.

"Darling, what if I'm shipped out right away? It'll be a long time before we'll see each other again if I go overseas."

He slipped an arm around her waist and they walked over to the glass case filled with ivories. They remained standing.

"Scott, why did we get news of my brother's death just at the time we were leaving for Nevada?"

"Darling, it was only a horrible coincidence."

"Do you really believe that?" she asked.

"Of course, Lin," he answered.

"Scott, I don't."

His voice was like one soothing a child: "Darling, darling, of course it was."

He made her sit down. He asked again: "Lin, will you leave with me tomorrow?"

To think was difficult and he had broken her train of thought. "Scott, let me think," she pleaded. With an effort she concentrated again. Now there was no doubt in her mind why the telegram had arrived just as she and Scott were leaving for Nevada. She let out a cry and covered her face with her hands.

Scott lifted her from the chair and held her tightly. "Darling, I shouldn't be asking you now. We'll talk tonight."

"Scott, I'm sorry, I'm sorry. I can't see you tonight."

"I just want to talk with you. I just want to be with you. I won't ask you to leave."

"Scott, you don't understand."

"Darling, I do. I promise you I won't ask you to leave. I'll wait for you to say it."

She started to protest again but his mouth was on hers, and then for the moment all that mattered to her was this closeness. Her fingers pressed hard on his back when he withdrew to speak. "No! Don't say anything," she said. He touched the hairpins in her chignon, reminding both of them of their days last autumn.

"Scott," she cried, "we have our days in Berkeley to remember."

"Darling, we could have them again," he said.

She knew he waited for an answer. But she could not say what he wanted to hear. With great tenderness she kissed him, then pulled away and looked at him.

The silence was broken when he asked, "Darling, are you all right?"

After a while she said: "Scott, I must go upstairs to change my dress. Stay here so I can see you from the door."

Her hand was on the doorknob when she called to him: "Scott, it was wrong that we ever fell in love. I will never see you again," and before he could reach her, she was gone.

LIKE THE OLD SCHOLAR IN HIS MOUNTAIN RETREAT IN the monochrome painting, Lin passed her days in the House of Tong. When she talked to visitors it was of charming stories as unreal as the world she lived in now. She told them how the deep red of the *sang de bœuf* had been finally achieved. In desperation the potter had entered the furnace himself so that the emperor's order for a vase the color of blood could be delivered. She told them of one of the Eight Immortals, the humble woman of the seventh century who, because she was filial, gained immortality with the aid of powdered pearls and moonbeams.

She told them of the Yin and the Yang; that the Yang represented life, light, righteousness, the visible world, gods and the male element; that the Yin represented death, darkness, secretiveness, evil demons, the invisible world and the female element; and that according to the ancient Chinese those two elements, though conflicting, are always necessary to make a perfect whole.

At nights when she could not sleep, she sat by the

window of her bedroom and thought of Scott. Always the words came back to her: "Please let me see you. This is my last day in town," to which she had answered nothing, her finger pushing down on the telephone receiver. In the stillness of the night she would lay her head on her arms and cry. Then, lifting her head up, any doubt that she had been wrong in sending Scott away would vanish.

At times the studio became unbearable. Then she would call Val and together they would set up their easels and canvas chairs somewhere and paint. At her insistence they would turn home even before a hint of twilight began to show.

When the burden of her guilt was less heavy she went alone to the park across the street from where she lived. There as she sat and painted she would retrace her last day with Scott. Always the remembrance of the telegram would renew her guilt. She would run home and find that the children she had sketched had evil, ugly faces and the tall sprawling tree was like a treacherous hand.

One day, in another part of town, she painted the weeping willows by a lake. A procession of ducks swam in the water, making a wide V behind them as they swam. After an hour she stopped and closed her eyes. In her mind she saw a finished painting of the willows and the lake, then opened her eyes to the results of her own work. How the two differed! What she could see in her mind would never be the reality. She could paint a hundred canvasses but the willow tree would never be as sad and beautiful in her painting as she saw it.

The sun would be setting soon. She prepared to leave before the sky changed colors. In her task of gathering up tubes and brushes, and disassembling her easel and chair, she was caught when the first ray of pink appeared. Since Scott had left, she had always hated the evening. Then the single horizontal ray of pink expanded and glowed deeper. Soon a shadow of blue came behind and the spectacle of the sky made her breathless.

"Was it as beautiful as this in Berkeley?" she asked herself; and she answered herself, "Yes, it was."

Then as the pink turned darker, soon to be gray, her mind returned to that unhappy Sunday. Her eyes were on the single streak of pink remaining in the sky as she thought: Perhaps it was as Scott had said. It had been a horrible coincidence, but only a coincidence, that the message had arrived when they were leaving for Nevada. Like the painting in the mind against the painting by the hand, what she had dreaded was not the reality. Her thoughts came in fragments, too delicate now to probe further, but she knew that soon they would come to her complete. Now the sky was dark. She thought no more as she packed her paint box and picked up her canvas chair.

The fragment of thought that came with the sunset had been the first fragile thread of the cocoon. Time strengthened the thread, now weaving day by day. She no longer sat by the window and cried. She was no longer afraid of the evening. The children she sketched no longer looked evil and ugly. Her eyes were brighter; she felt in possession of herself again.

Soon she would write Scott about everything, but not yet. Would this new feeling continue, or would she wake up in the middle of the night and find that it had been the fleeting beauty of blossoms in the winter wind? Then early one August morning in the daily routine of picking up the mail from the floor of the studio, her hand reached underneath a pile of white envelopes to pick up a pink one. Opening it, she read the unfamiliar handwriting of Mrs. Hayes. Mrs. Hayes wrote as the Chaplain had written her: Scott had been killed in action in July in the Sicilian Campaign of Lieutenant General Patton's Seventh Army.

GENTLE SUNSHINE WAS ALL ABOUT AND A PLEASANTLY mild wind bore it company for it was Indian summer; in no other time of the year is San Francisco lovelier than in late September. A box of fresh sesame cookies was in Lin's hands and she stood on the corner of Grant Avenue and California Street waiting for the cable car coming up from the financial district on Montgomery Street.

Earlier in the morning Mrs. Hayes had telephoned, asking her to come up to her house and she had replied that she would be there at about one-thirty. Lin boarded the cable car and they ascended the steep hill, leaving the Chinese quarter. They passed Nob Hill, rolled on to Van Ness Avenue and she began looking at the numbers on the doors. Wrought-iron fences guarded even plots of grass and neat beds of bright flowers. The houses seemed serene under the benevolent protection of the sun. It was a beautiful day, but her heart was heavy.

The lovely yellow medallion of the wallpaper in the foyer was a contrast to the soft gray dress Mrs. Hayes wore.

This was only their second meeting but Mrs. Hayes greeted Lin as if she had always loved her, pressing her cheek to Lin's. Lin allowed her to do so for she knew with Mrs. Hayes's cheek to hers, that Mrs. Hayes thought of Scott.

They sat in front of the unlit fireplace, the Japanese vase above them on the mantel. Mrs. Hayes poured a cup of tea and Lin offered her the sesame cookies. Mrs. Hayes began: "Miss Kwong . . . Lin . . . may I call you Lin? Lin . . . let me tell you how dreadfully sorry I am that I . . ." Lin listened in silence while Mrs. Hayes went on, wondering if, were it not for death, would Mrs. Hayes be talking so. Yet she listened, for in so doing she helped Scott's mother to regain the relief of an unburdened conscience.

Mrs. Hayes finished and closed her eyes for a few seconds. Then wearily she got up and went to a secretary and took out an envelope from a drawer. She came over to Lin again and said: "Lin, some things of Scott's were sent back to me yesterday. Did you give him this?" It was the jade carp she had given him for his birthday. It swung delicately in the air, the red silk cord worn and dirty; how quickly Scott had adopted the habit of rubbing the cool jade with his fingers. Mrs. Hayes offered it to Lin and she accepted it.

"And Lin, there was a letter, an unfinished one. It didn't have your name but I'm very sure it was meant for you. I read only the first few lines." She handed Lin a letter, soiled and wrinkled, and Lin took it and, remembering their last day together, felt that now her heart must break.

She rose to leave. Once again Mrs. Hayes held her hands briefly. Lin walked through the house for the last time, the house where Scott had lived. Then suddenly

Mrs. Hayes asked: "You're not ill any more, are you, my dear?"

Lin stopped, turned, and looked at Mrs. Hayes. She said, "No, I'm not. But how did you ever know about that?"

Mrs. Hayes said, "The last time Scott wrote me he said that you were ill after you received news of your brother's death and that . . ."

And as she talked Lin knew that she would not be afraid to read Scott's letter. Scott had known—he had known all along.

Now no mild wind bore company with the sunshine and Lin walked in an unhurried pace in the warm afternoon. She would walk a little before taking the cable car. The street was quiet and empty. Suddenly from a distance she saw the tall, slender figure of a man whose hair was golden in the sunlight. She raised a hand and called, "Scott!" But it was not Scott; it would never be Scott, for Scott was dead. She stood still, her eyes closed, a hand on her mouth to quiet herself. The feeling that her flesh must surely tear out of her skin in longing for him came to her again. A mild wind blew and hovered over her; it seemed to her to be the gentle presence of Scott himself. She called out softly: "Scott, Scott, wasn't it good we knew the words of that poet. Wasn't it good!"

She walked on and the gentle wind followed her. "Scott, I haven't used my lilac for a long time but I'll wear it tonight when I read your letter."

The mild wind was gone. She called for it to return but it did not heed her. She started to cry again but she stopped. What good could it do? Cry to the heavens she might, but in the words of the old Chinese, it is easier to drag the bright moon out of the water than to restore a soul.

She walked on, her pace now less unhurried, letter and jade carp in hand. She boarded the cable car. It started its descent down the steep hill. She turned to face the view. Far off, the bay and the bridge were in sight, and in the background the hills of Berkeley, where a year ago she and Scott had walked.

She felt again a gentle wind as it followed her down the hill. The cable car came to a stop on level ground; the air was still once more. Suddenly the leaves of a sycamore tree trembled. A little robin flew away. A tear fell as she kept her eyes on the tree and in her heart she cried: "Goodbye, Scott, goodbye."